Crazy Dog and the Wolf

By

Dorothy Eckhart Smith

DEDICATED TO

My brother, John, whose character is much

the same as that of Dog; and to Duff, our

collie, who, I am sure, is a direct

descendant of Puppy, the wolf.

About the Author

Born in New York City, and raised in Seattle, WA, author Dorothy Eckhart Smith was given a book about prehistoric people while in second grade. She became fascinated with early humans and read everything she could find about them. As a young woman in the 1930s, Dorothy wrote and illustrated Crazy Dog and the Wolf.

A woman of varied interests and imagination, Dorothy continued to develop her artistic skills. She was the lead colorist for the photography department of Fredrick Nelson, a Marshall Field's subsidiary in Seattle, WA. She was a columnist for the Yakima Our Times and has also been published in other periodicals.

She married Bill Smith, and they raised six children in Yakima, WA, all of whom grew up enchanted with the story of Crazy Dog and the Wolf.

Table of Contents

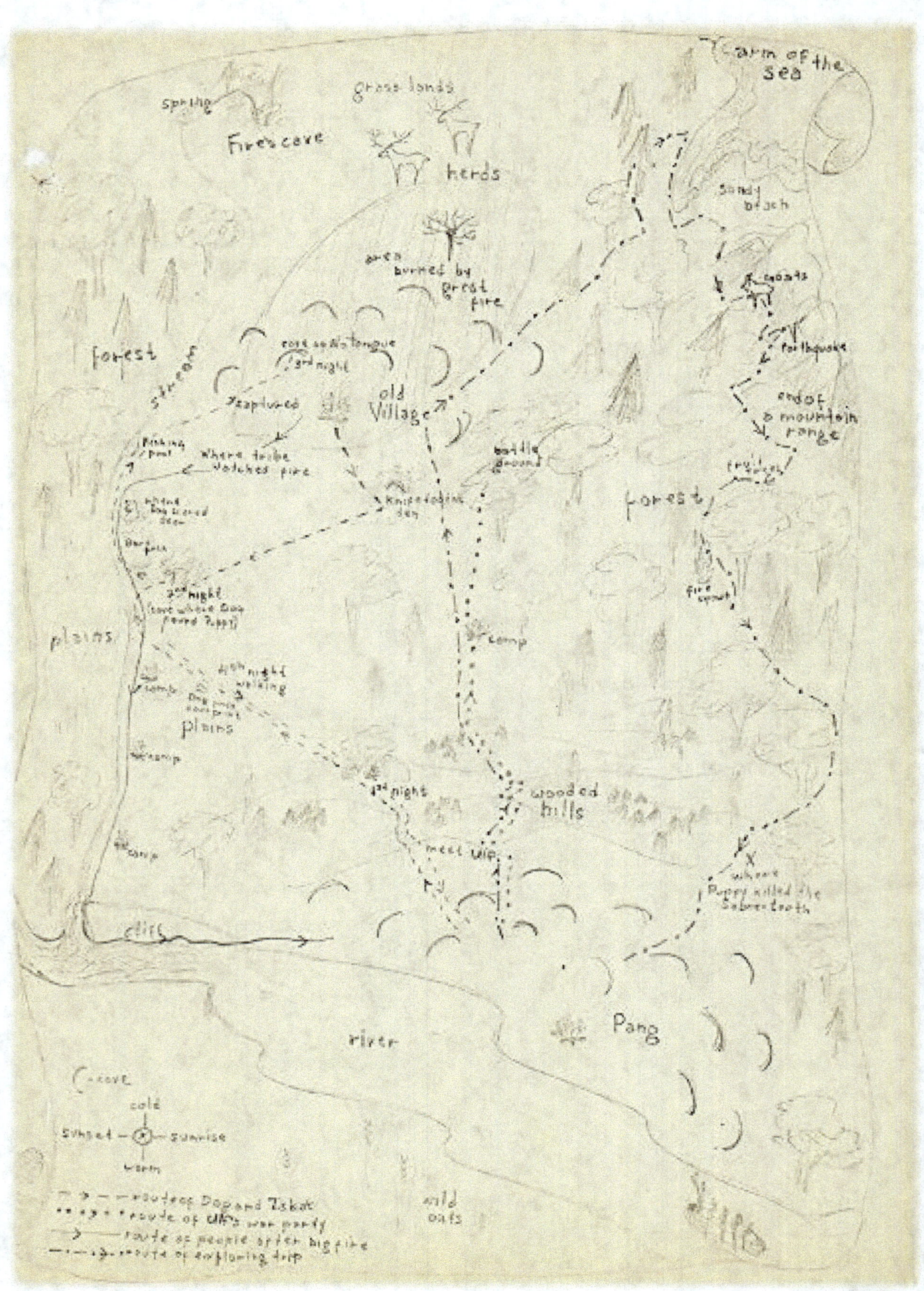
arm of the sea
grass lands
spring
Firescove
herds
sandy beach
area burned by great fire
goats
earthquake
forest
stream
rose scale tongue
3rd night
end of a mountain range
recaptured
old Village
battle ground
trail
forests
fishing pool
where tribe watched fire
Knife-tooth's den
island boy crossed sea
fire spout
rapids
3rd night
cave where dog saved Puppi
camp
4th night walking
dog finds our print
camp
plains
plains
camp
3rd night
meet Ulf
wooded hills
camp
X where Puppi killed the Sabre-tooth
cliff
river
Pang
wild oats
cove
cold
sunset
sunrise
warm
route of Dop and Tiskat
route of Ulf's war party
route of people after big fire
route of exploring trip

Chapter One:
Puppy

This is a story of a boy named Dog who lived a very long time ago. He was a Cro-Magnon boy, which means he lived in a cave, and his clothes were made from the skins of animals. Dog belonged to the tribe of Pang, one of the last Cro-Magnon tribes. Though, there were other races of cavemen, and Dog knew some of them.

Dog was a cheerful nine-year-old boy. He couldn't read, write, or spell, but he knew how to hunt animals, what the birdcalls meant, how to find his way through the trackless forest, and many other things.

Dog's mother's name was Sand, and Dog thought she was very beautiful. She had long, red hair, which she tied together at the back of her neck with a bit of animal hide. Her skin was rough and coarse, but her eyes were kind, which is probably why Dog loved her so much.

Ulf, Dog's father, thought she was beautiful too. He was a huge man and a mighty hunter. He was the chief of the Pang tribe because he was a brave man who knew how to kill the mammoth and saber-toothed tiger. Ulf was Dog's only teacher, and the lessons he taught his son were about the animals and the forest so Dog could be a mighty hunter and a good chief someday. Ulf always wore carved bear teeth around his neck to show he was chief. The necklace had been made by the first chieftain, old Pang, and was handed down to each chief after him as a badge of leadership. Other men had killed bears and made necklaces, but none had carved designs on the teeth out of respect.

It was a morning in spring when Ulf brought home a great wolf. Sand had been very joyful because the wolf meant a great many things to her. Dog's bed, which was a pile of leaves and furs, needed a new cover. This could be now made from the wolf's hide. The family needed food, so Sand cut parts of the wolf's flesh and put them in a hollow stone half filled with water. She then heated small stones in the fire and put them into the water to make it boil. It was a very slow way to cook, but it was the only way she had. Ulf and Dog thought the meat was delicious. Sand dried what they didn't eat and put it away for winter when food would be scarce. She cleaned the bones and made needles, scrapers, and many other implements from them, and from the strong sinews, she made thread and string.

"Dog," said Ulf as they squatted around the fire and enjoyed their meal, "this wolf has a cub. I want you to go and get it. Be careful, though, the wolf cub is very tender."

"Yes, Father, but where is it?"

"Follow the Laughing Stream downhill, until you come to the bare rock. A little way toward the sunrise, and you will find her den. Hurry now, and don't stop to play."

Dog started out on his journey, singing as he walked. It made him feel very important to have such a responsibility, almost as though he were a man! He thought about how a man should act, making him realize how silly he was behaving. Men didn't sing and warn the animals of their approach. Men crept and looked about them carefully with their weapons ready. Dog poised his little spear, glanced in all directions, and crept furtively through the underbrush. He was a man, stalking a saber-toothed tiger!

It was a long way down the stream. Dog was soon hungry and very warm, but he kept on until he found a place where the stream backwatered and formed a still, deep pool. There, he stopped and plunged his face into the cool water. It felt good, and Dog stayed there as long as possible. He wished he could leave his face in the pool all day, but he sat up very suddenly when a fish brushed against him. *What a silly fish!* Dog thought. He leaned over the edge of the pool and stuck his tongue out in hopes that the fish would see the gesture.

Dog leaned over the pool and stuck his tongue
out at it, in hopes that the fish would see it.

"You just wait," he said, "you'll be sorry." He turned away to gather some dry moss and sticks and built a fire. Dog was glad to have his flint and stone. He carried them in a little fur pouch at his side. It didn't take him long to strike the two together and make a spark, which fell into the pile of moss. He blew and fanned it until he had a merry little flame at the pool's edge.

"Wait," he cautioned the fire and turned to the pool, plunging his arm deep into the water. Then, quickly, his hand was out again, holding onto a large, fat fish. Laughing at it, Dog had no doubt that it was the same fish. It certainly did look very upset.

"Didn't I tell you you would be sorry? Now I am going to eat you, and you will never bump another little boy!" Dog very calmly cut off the fish's head and tail with his flint knife. A forked stick wasn't hard to find, and neither was a twig to use to fasten the fish to the shaft. In a short time, lunch was cooking, and it smelled so good Dog's stomach began to growl like a bear.

Dog considered himself an excellent cook, so he lingered to enjoy each bite of his late enemy despite the need to hurry. After he had appeased his angry stomach, Dog discovered he was tired. He decided he would lie down for just a moment before he went on his way.

A wolf passed by, but his stomach was full, and he was old and lazy. A deer came to the pool's edge and drank, unafraid. The fiery mammoth-sized light that was the sun moved from over the treetops until it was directly above Dog before he yawned and sat up.

"I've been asleep! What if an animal had come? I better not tell Father I was asleep. He'd say such a careless boy could never make a good chief. I must hurry now!" So, Dog, thoroughly frightened and ashamed of himself, ran through the brush as fast as he could. Any animal that strayed to his sleeping place would find a strange stick with a piece of stone attached… Dog had forgotten his spear!

Dog stopped only once in the late afternoon to eat some berries he found growing close to the stream's edge. They weren't very ripe, but they tasted good, and Dog wasn't very particular. He ate all he could, and then filled his pouch and started again. He was quite adept at tossing a bit of food into the air and catching it in his mouth as it fell. In this manner, he ate the rest of the berries as he traveled. Once, when he opened his mouth, a tiny insect flew in, but he ate it right along with the berry and didn't mind a bit.

The sun was beginning to color the sky when Dog reached the huge bare rock that marked the turning point in his trail. He was glad to get there because dark shadows were already creeping among the trees. He planned to sleep in the wolf's den and start home the next morning. The sun was going to sleep, so it was hard to see in the dim light, and Dog would have walked right past the den if he hadn't heard a small, lonesome whimper. He looked and saw the cub at the entrance. His search was over, and Dog was a happy, if hungry, little boy.

"Stay there a short while, little cub. I am going after bird eggs. I'll be right back." Dog loved eggs, and he gathered a whole pouch full before he returned to the cub. It was late evening when he got his fire built in front of the den. Only then did he turn to survey the baby wolf. The cub was cold and snuggled close to Dog and shivered. He was very young and soft, so Dog let him stay near while he prepared to cook his eggs on the hot rocks around the fire. After one had sizzled a minute, Dog slid his knife under it and transferred it quickly from the rock to his mouth. It was good, but Dog's sigh of contentment was interrupted by a cold little nose pushing against his elbow. The cub was looking at him with its appealing eyes.

"Hungry?" asked Dog. It was shameful--the son of a chief being so concerned about an animal--but Dog couldn't look away from those eyes. "I must have the head sickness," he said as he broke one of the eggs into his hand and held it out to the cub, who lapped it up and begged for more. Dog gave him several eggs. Even though Dog was not quite full, he curled up into the leaves on the den's floor with the cub burrowed close beside him. He patted the cub's head and made a comforting, clucking noise.

"Pup – pup – pup – don't worry – pup - Pup! That's a fine name for you–Puppy! We'll be all right here with my spear for protection. My spear!" Dog sat up and realized–his spear was gone! "Oh, Puppy, what can I do? I've lost my spear, and I'm afraid. We might have to stay here all night without a spear! How did you manage last night without anything? You are a brave little cub, braver than I am, I guess. You didn't even have a fire! If you can be so brave, then I can too. Come on, let's go to sleep." The sun had barely begun its daily stroll when Dog sat up and rubbed his eyes. It took him several minutes to remember where he was, but when Puppy crawled up on his lap, the adventures of the day before all came back to him.

"I'm hungry," he said, "how about you, Puppy? Want more eggs?" Puppy wagged his tail and grinned. Dog was sure he was saying he loved eggs and would be very happy if Dog found some.

After breakfast, they started toward Pang, Puppy perched on Dog's shoulder. Bare rock invited them to take a nap in the sun, but Dog turned his back on it and kept to the stream. Soon they came to the berry patch, and Dog stopped to pick some berries because cave boys were always ready to eat.

The wolf cub didn't like berries, but Dog did, and so did bears. Dog was about to put a huge and very ripe berry into his mouth when a big black bear suddenly stood up on the other side of the bush. Dog dropped his berry, but he found he couldn't run. They looked at each other for several minutes, and then Dog yelled, "Boo!" The bear, surprised, sat back on its haunches, turned, and ran away from the patch as fast as his fat legs could go.

Dog looked after the bear. "Puppy! We chased him away! By the great sun mammoth, wait 'til Father hears this!" He picked Puppy up, danced a couple of happy steps, and then raced off down the trail.

"Puppy, look! There is my spear beside the pool!" Dog picked up the spear. It hadn't been touched at all. "Nobody has been here, Puppy. I'm glad I found this. Now Father will never know how careless I was. I can catch another fish."

There was no nap for Dog that day. He was anxious for Ulf and Sand to see his cub and to tell them how he chased the bear. The last lap of the trip was a happy one. Dog ran, danced, and answered the birdcalls. When he was hot, he waded in the stream and splashed water on Puppy, who ran along the bank and made fierce, mock growls at the tingling cold drops. As the two neared the village of Pang, Dog sang to Puppy of his adventures. Here are the words of his song:

At night the wolves howl.

It is dark, and I am afraid.

My spear is gone, my fire dim.

It is cold.

Day comes, and I am happy.

The sun-mammoth warms me.

I frighten the great bear.

O, I am a mighty hunter!

Feel the cool stream against my feet!

Though Dog knew no real song, he sang whatever words came into his head and didn't even bother to make them rhyme. His voice carried to the village, where Jet heard him coming at last.

Jet was a little girl and Dog's best friend. She was only eight but was as brown and sturdy as Dog. She was dressed in several small pelts that had been sewn together. It looked the same as Dog's garment but much softer.

Jet was very proud of it. Her curly hair was longer than Dog's, and the curls hung every which way on her head.

"Dog! Dog!" she called as she ran toward his voice.

"I hear you, Jet," he answered and came running to meet her. "Look at the wolf cub! My father wanted me to bring him home to eat, but I am going to keep him!"

"Keep him!? Oh, Dog, he will grow into a wolf and eat you!"

"No, Jet, I don't think so. Do you remember that man the hunters found a long time ago? He had grown up alone in the woods, and he scratched and fought just like an animal."

"Yes, I remember. But what does that have to do with the cub?"

"Well, if a man growing up with animals is wild, why wouldn't an animal growing up with men be tame, if we are kind to it?"

"Yes, you're right! May I hold him? What is his name?"

"Puppy. Come on, let's tell Ulf and Sand."

Sand looked up as the two children raced toward her. She had been scraping the wolf's hide, but she stopped to listen when she saw how excited they were.

"Mother, look! Here is the cub, and I want to keep him!"

"What? Ulf, come here! Dog says he wants to keep the cub! He talks as though he were crazy!"

 "Keep the cub?" asked Ulf, coming out of the cave. "Dog, I am surprised at you. He is a wolf, and wolves are very fierce!"

"I want to tame him, Father, so he won't be so fierce. Please let me!"

Ulf and Sand looked at each other, and Ulf shook his head very slowly. Then he said, "Tell me the rest of your adventures, son."

"I stayed all night in the wolf's den, and the next day I chased a great bear away from a berry patch without even my spear! Oh!" Dog clapped his hand over his mouth. His secret was out!

"Where was your spear, son? Answer me, Dog."

"It–it was by the fishing pool."

"What was it doing there?"

"I–I fell asleep." Dog wished Jet would go home. He was very ashamed and did not want Jet to hear his father scold him.

"Fell asleep!"

"Yes, Father, and when I woke up, I forgot my spear."

"Oh Dog, how could a son of mine be so careless? Fell asleep in the woods and forgot your spear. I don't know what could be the matter with you. Tell me about the bear."

"I just yelled at it, and it ran away."

Ulf put his hand to his forehead. "My son, don't you know such a thing is impossible? And taming a wolf is impossible too. I hate to say this, but I think demons have taken your mind."

"But Father, it's all true! I did scare the bear, and I can tame the wolf."

"All right, you may keep the cub. Run and play now." Ulf turned to Sand and said, "I'm sure he has the head sickness, and we must humor him. Someday when the cub is bigger, I will kill it in secret, and we can tell Dog it ran away. As a cub, it is harmless and makes Dog happy."

Meanwhile, Dog, Jet, and Puppy were sitting farther down the glade. "Jet, do you think I have the head sickness?"

"No, Dog. I believe you, and so will they when Puppy is grown up and tame."

Soon everyone in their village knew that Dog, the son of Ulf, had a head sickness. Certain jealous-minded ladies believed bad luck had visited Ulf because he had chosen Sand, whom he had to steal from an enemy village, instead of one of them. Jet became Dog's only playmate because the boys all yelled at him and chased him away. At times Dog thought of finding himself a cave far away where he and Puppy could live in peace. Once, he even went so far as to tell Jet of his plan and asked her to come along, but when he went home, his parents were so kind to him that he decided to stay a while longer.

In this manner, much time passed, and Puppy grew while Ulf and Sand kept saying, "Tomorrow–tomorrow, we will kill the wolf." But as the days passed and Puppy never turned on Dog, they didn't take action. Ulf and Sand would have died before they would admit it, but they rather liked the big animal who wagged his tail and was so good a guard for Dog's new little brother.

Dog, Jet, and Puppy were three small friends who thought everyone believed Dog was crazy. But they were wrong.

Chapter Two:
The Big Fire

It was late summer--the Season of Dry Grasses--a little over a year since Dog upset the village by bringing home a wolf cub and keeping it. Ulf and Sand were discussing a name for Dog's little brother. He had lived for many months without one, and Sand was growing tired of calling him just Baby. Dog was named Dog because Sand liked the sound of the syllable. When Dog's mother was a child, she liked to play on the sandy creek near her home, and the people took to calling her Sand. It seemed all the new baby did was cry, sleep, and eat. There was no name in those activities.

"Look," said Dog, pointing toward where the baby lay on a bearskin outside the cave, "how he waves his hand toward the sky and laughs."

"He likes the sky," said Ulf.

"Perhaps he would like to be named after it," Sand looked at Ulf, "Do you think so?

"Sky? Yes, we shall call him Sky! Dog, run and tell everyone I have decided my second son shall be named Sky."

"Sky! Sky! Sky!" Dog shouted as he ran to Jet's cave. Together they visited every cave in the village to tell the people of the name for Dog's little brother. So intent were they that they did not notice the rising wind until they were on the way back to Dog's cave.

"I don't want to go home," said Jet, "the wind is blowing strong and cold."

"Stay," invited Sand, "and eat with us. Your mother knows you are with Dog."

A little while later, a returning hunter looked in the cave. "The wild animals are hurrying to shelter. Better take your fire in!" he called and went on to the next cave.

Ulf made a torch and lit the end. He then put out the fire at the entrance to the cave. The Pang tribe had seen forest fires start through the wind blowing these small flames about. Sand hastily piled some dry logs in one corner of the cave. Right above it was a wide crack in the wall that went clear up to the top so that one could see a streak of daylight through it. Ulf lit the wood before he noticed where she had piled it. Then he yelled.

"Why did you put the wood there? Might as well be outside! You may move it someplace else yourself." Ulf stalked across the cave, sat down, and looked the other way. Sand looked at the fire.

"Look, Ulf! The smoke!" She exclaimed.

"That's the worst of wind storms," said Ulf, "Fires are inside, and the cave fills with smoke."

"But Ulf–the smoke is going up the crack!"

Ulf looked. Sure enough, the smoke was being drawn out of the cave, and the air was clear.

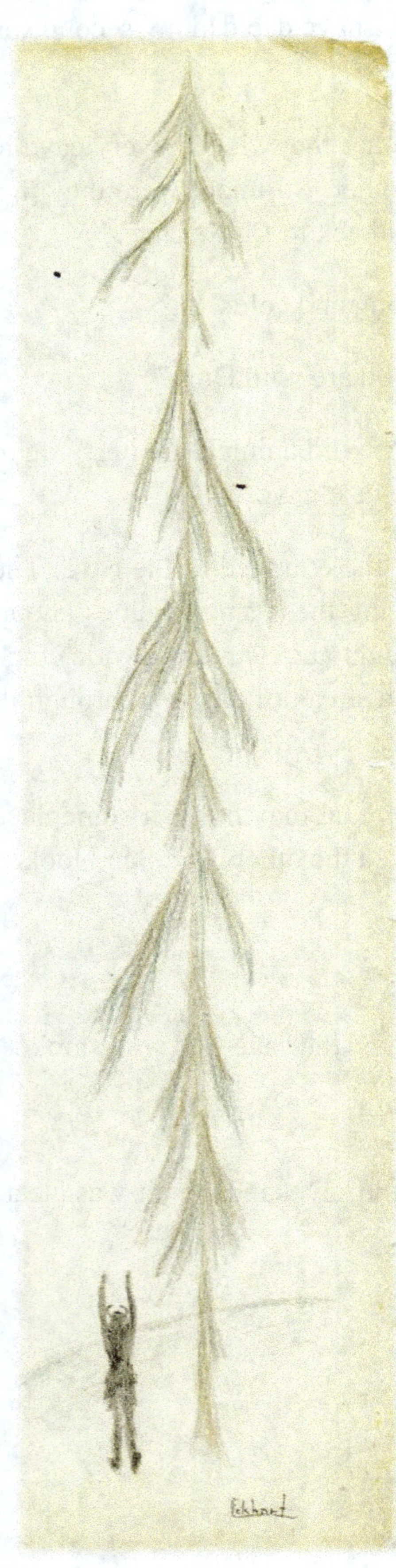

"We have discovered a great magic," said Ulf.

"We?" questioned Sand. "It was I. You wouldn't even look at it."

"Well, all right. But anyhow, we have the secret here, and we must thank the fire spirit for showing us how to guide the smoke."

Dog ran in from the entrance, where he had been watching the wind.

"Father! The fire spirit has come with the wind! I saw one of his flashes! He is angry at the tribe of Pang!"

Ulf ran to the front of the cave and saw the lightning. "Maybe the spirit is angry because we found the crack and sent the smoke up through it. Sand–quick–move the fire!"

Even as he spoke, a bolt struck a tree, and it fell near the center of the village. Immediately every stick of wood near it was aflame, and the people were running from their caves into the woods.

Ulf spoke, "The tree was guided away from the cave of Ulf. Our secret is good. But we must hurry before the great fire reaches us!"

Ulf grabbed as many furs as he could and gave them to Jet and Dog. Sand picked little Sky up and put him in a little skin that she tied across her back. In her hands, she carried her bone tools and some dried meat. Ulf took his weapons and, followed by Puppy, the family fled before the sweeping flames reached their cave.

They met other families as they ran. Nobody knew where they were going, but they seemed to naturally follow the course of the stream downhill. Puppy was as afraid as his people, but he stuck close to them. This was the first test of his tameness and loyalty, and he came through. Puppy was no longer a wolf.

Farther and farther they ran. They were a long way from the fire before they stopped to rest. The tribe of Pang watched the bright sky that showed where their homes were burning. The fire spirit must have been very angry indeed to drive them away like that.

All through the night, they watched. Those that had had time to bring furs and food divided them among the rest of the people, and the children were wrapped up to sleep.

As Ulf watched the flames, his thoughts were many and troubled. Why had the medicine man not prevented this calamity? Why did he not even warn the people that it was coming? What had angered the fire spirit? Ulf could not find the answers to these questions even though he pondered all night. The medicine man had seemed as frightened as anyone. It was very odd. Now the medicine man was asleep on two of the finest furs in the village, asleep when he should have been directing a rain dance! Ulf looked at him, shrugged, and turned his attention to the wall of flame. The wind was gone, but still, the fire crept slowly toward the little group of cavemen. If it would only rain!

Puppy lay at Ulf's feet, and as Ulf thought, he absent-mindedly rubbed the animal's ears. The wolf knew that this man loved him, even though he did his best to hide it. It was the love of these humans that kept Puppy from running wild that night. Toward morning he did slip away, but Ulf didn't notice it. Ulf had fallen asleep sitting up, watching the fire. Dog noticed Puppy's absence quickly enough when he awoke.

"Father! Puppy is gone! Where did he go?"

Ulf didn't know, and he was worried. "We can't go and hunt him, Dog. It would be no use. He is a wolf, and has probably caught up with the other animals now. He was afraid of the big fire."

"But Father, Puppy learned to love the warm fire in our cave."

"That was just a little fire, Dog. This is a big one and probably brought the wild animal fear back into his heart. It can't be helped, Dog." Dog, even though he was a mighty hunter and the son of the chief, was crying. He tried not to, but the thought of never seeing Puppy again was too much for him.

All day the fire burned, and the people watched it. Dog and Jet sat and talked about Puppy. They remembered how he played, his big grin when he was pleased, the way he growled if anyone tried to touch little Sky. The other children laughed at them. "Crazy Dog!" they yelled. "Crazy Dog couldn't tame the wolf! Yaaaaa!"

Suddenly the children stopped shouting and slunk back to their parents. Something had frightened them. "I wonder," began Dog, then stopped. Something warm and wet was against his ear. Cautiously he raised his hand and touched–fur. It was Puppy! He had crept up behind Dog and was licking his ear.

Puppy! Dog hugged him, and he and the great beast rolled over and over in the grass. Puppy was whining, and crying, and barking all at once. That was probably the first real bark ever heard by these people. It showed how completely the wolf had changed. He didn't howl anymore.

It was Sand who noticed why Puppy had gone. She saw a dead field bird!

A large, fat bird that Puppy had roamed far to find because the wildlife had all fled before the fire. The people were hungry, and the dried meat was gone, so the bird was a huge stroke of luck for Dog and his family. Ulf decided all the children should share the bird because grown-up stomachs could stand more hunger than little ones.

Sand was preparing the bird when the medicine man's wife came over to her. "Fire is hungry," she said.

"But it's for the children."

"I don't care. Fire is hungry." Fire's wife was a large, flat-faced woman. She had neither the brains nor the looks of Sand and was jealous. Sand was the wife of the chief, but she would have to give up the bird to the medicine man, for he was magic. "Give," she said and held out her hand. Sand sighed and gave the fowl to the woman, who grinned and waddled away with it.

"Why our witch doctor would have to pick such a wife," muttered Sand, but Ulf put his hand over her mouth. One might think such things but never think them aloud! At that moment, Ulf was wondering why Fire did not call a rain dance. He saw Fire was too busy eating, and Ulf was very disgusted.

When Fire finished his meal, he lay down on the soft furs and went to sleep. Would he never call on the rain god? Then Ulf felt a drop on his nose–and another–and another! He stood up and breathed deeply. The harsh smoke smell was disappearing. Rain had come! Soon it was pouring, and the people shouted, danced, and held their arms up to it. In spite of Fire, the rain spirit had seen them and had brought relief! Puppy rolled in the soggy grass and bit at it while the people danced. Finally, everyone picked up their belongings and prepared to go home.

"No," said Ulf, "our homes are ruined. The grass and trees are burnt. The animals have gone away, and hunting will be very poor. Let us go on downstream and find a new home." The people agreed and followed Ulf. Only two families decided to go back, and the tribe of Pang never saw them again.

Downstream they went. They were hungry and cold, but their homes were behind them, and they had to keep going. At night they stopped and built a campfire, and one of the men kept watch. Once, they caught a small animal that wasn't more than a mouthful for each person. They lived mostly on not-quite-ripe nuts. They passed the place where Dog frightened the bear and the place where he found Puppy, but how different this trip was from the other!

They went downstream for several days, and Dog noticed the creek was widening. He, Jet, and Puppy ran on ahead to see where it was going. It curled among the rocks, and then, a little way ahead, the children heard a great roar. Jet was afraid. She thought it might be some huge animal, but Dog was scornful of her. If it were a beast, he could hide, but he wanted to go and see. Jet was a brave little girl, so, in spite of her fear, she followed Dog and Puppy.

"Look, Jet. If it were something to be afraid of, Puppy would be bristling his neck fur. Come on, it's all right." The three crawled through the underbrush until they found a tiny waterfall. The stream was tumbling headlong into a raging river!

Here they waited for the rest of the tribe, and when the people arrived, they stared in awe at the river. "Upstream," said Ulf, "through that narrow gorge!"

Fire objected. "The rocks are slippery from this rain."

"Upstream," repeated Ulf. "Have we a coward for a medicine man?"

Fire looked at Ulf for a minute, then grunted. The people started upstream.

They were in a valley now, which became narrower and narrower. Soon the tribesmen had to tie their burdens on their backs and cling to the slippery rocks with their hands. One man stood up and took a step. He slipped and fell into the river, where he was battered against the sharp rocks and drowned. The rest didn't look back. Such a thing might happen to any of them, and they were busy protecting themselves.

Ulf felt very foolish as he stopped every once in a while to help Dog and Jet with Puppy. The wolf was having a hard time. His claws could find no hold in the bare rocks, and he would have slipped if Dog and Jet had not hung on to his wet fur, for it was still raining.

What seemed like hours later, the gorge began to widen and slope a bit. The river ran slower, and before they even realized it, they were in a very pleasant valley. The river ran slow and wide through the center, and the slopes and foothills were dotted with caves. Nut-bearing trees and berry bushes grew there, and on the other side of the river grew tall yellow grasses.

"I wonder if the people will welcome us," wondered Sand. She was very anxious to find a dry place where little Sky could get warm.

Ulf went to the nearest cave and called out. When he got no answer, he looked in. It was empty. Hastily, he called all the men together, and each investigated a cave. When they reported to Ulf, he was amazed. None of the men had found a soul. The village was deserted.

"I wonder what could have made them go. There was no fire here," said Ulf. Fire thought there might have been a plague, but the men had found no dead bodies. There were always dead left after a plague. No, there had been another reason.

"Let's not stand here in the rain," said Sand. "I want a home. Are there any caves with cracks in the walls that you can see daylight through?"

The men were astonished at her question. But she was the chief's wife and should be pleased. "Yes, several. One over there by that oak tree, one here by the river, and one back behind the berry patch." Sand studied all three and chose the largest and finest one, the one behind the oak tree.

Fire and his wife had already taken a very large cave near the center of the village. After that, the rest of the people scurried around and found caves for themselves. The new Village of Pang was established.

That evening Fire called the people to do a thanksgiving dance to please the spirits and call their goodwill to the tribe. The tribe had no great fire because it was still raining but at the entrance of each cave that night, a small flame burned where it would be sheltered.

During the night, the rain stopped, and the morning sun helped dry the dripping world. Ulf and his hunters went out and had rare good luck. The animals had not been hunted for quite some time in this area and were unafraid of the men. The next day some of the men went out alone, while others stayed home to help cure meat. Toward evening they had all returned except Leaf, and he was nowhere to be found. A few days later, Snail, a little baby, wandered off and did not come back. They believed whatever was happening to their missing tribesmen was the reason for the deserted village.

One day, Dog was playing in the woods alone. The men were at the council, Puppy was watching over Sky, and Jet was learning how to dry meat. Luckily Dog was not singing or crashing through the bushes, for suddenly, he stood quite still, and his heart almost stopped beating. The wind was blowing toward him, so the main thing to do was remain quiet. He burrowed into the grass and crept slowly, though he longed to scream and run. Wind–don't change! Wind–keep blowing this way! Slowly Dog crept, expecting every moment to be his last. Then he reached the edge of the clearing. Jumping up, he ran into the center of the council shouting, "Saber-tooth! Saber-tooth!"

At the cry, mothers gathered their children into the caves and put more wood on the fires. The men reached for their weapons. Then one threw down his spear and laughed. "This boy is crazy! People who have the head sickness always see things that are not there." At his words, the men laughed nervously and began to throw down their weapons.

"Head of an ape!" yelled Ulf, "My son knows what he sees. The tiger is what got Snail and Leaf! It is why the other cowardly tribe left. We will kill the saber–toothed tiger. Come!"

They started following Dog and Puppy, who joined the party. Dog sighted the tiger. He was asleep. Cautiously the men surrounded the great animal who awoke as soon as a man got in the path of the wind! With a snarl, he faced the ring of people. He prepared to leap, but an arrow shot in his shoulder stopped him. With a roar, he wheeled, but his second leap was foiled by Puppy, who had broken loose from Dog's clutches. Ordinarily, a wolf alone would not attack a saber-toothed tiger, but the cat's wound and the dog's fierce loyalty to the boy made the match even.

Puppy landed squarely on the tiger's back and bit. With a yell of pain, the big cat shook him loose, but the wolf was back again. The men all took to the trees to watch, fascinated, this terrible battle– the first cat and dog fight they had ever seen. The animals reared up toward each other's throats. Both failed. Puppy got a hold on the cat's forepaw, but he let go and was around to its flank before the tiger had time to turn. He knew these holds were valueless, and so he didn't keep them. He was after the backbone. The hideous saber-toothed tiger raked Puppy's flank, but he jumped on the tiger's back. He knew he could win if he could stay there.

His strong jaws ground toward the cat's backbone. The tiger yelled and jumped, pawing the air, but Puppy hung on. His wolf nature told him he had the vital hold, and he must not let go!

Again, the tiger jumped and nearly dislocated the wolf's jaw, but this was a fight to the end, and Puppy did not let go. He dared not let go. Puppy had attacked the cat because he was tame and wanted to protect the little boy who was his master. Now he was fighting because his wild instincts had kicked in during the fight. He was killing for the sheer love of the kill. Puppy's jaws worked steadily and mercilessly. The great saber-toothed tiger, who had listened to the death yells of so many of his victims, was now screeching his own. The tiger jumped again, and in midair, his bones snapped, and he fell dead.

Puppy lay panting beside the huge carcass. The men were afraid he had turned wolf again, but Dog knew better. The bloodlust was gone from his eyes, and all he wanted was his master's praise. Dog slid out of the tree, went over to Puppy, and patted his head. Gathering courage, the rest of the men came down and prepared to haul the dead animal to the village.

"The skin is yours, Dog," said Ulf, "But you must give the tail to Fire."

The women of Pang were glad when they heard the victorious shouts of the men and saw the bright orange beast hanging from a pole. Puppy was in the lead, his wounds forgotten. He and Dog were heroes that day, to themselves anyhow.

The women were glad when they heard the victorious shouts of the men, and saw the bright orange beast hanging from the pole.

Sand was particularly pleased when the tiger was brought to her cave. She thought Ulf killed it. Dog cut the tail off and gave it to Fire, then told the story of the fight. When he finished, Sand looked disappointed, but Fire beamed, "Why should you have the skin? You didn't kill it. Nobody did, therefore, I should have the pelt."

"No," said Ulf. He was the only man who dared cross the witch doctor, and he did it often. "The wolf killed it, and the wolf belongs to Dog. It is Dog's fur!"

Again, the two men looked at each other silently, and again Fire was subdued. He picked up the tail and went to his own cave.

Dog decided the skin was to be used to make a bed for little Sky, and Sand and Jet were very proud of him for it. The head of the tiger Dog kept and sat upon a shelf in the cave where it glared down as if to tell the world of its untimely end. Dog was very fond of it.

That night around the council fire, Ulf sang and acted the story of the kill, and all the hunters danced. This is the way they celebrated the complete winning of their new home.

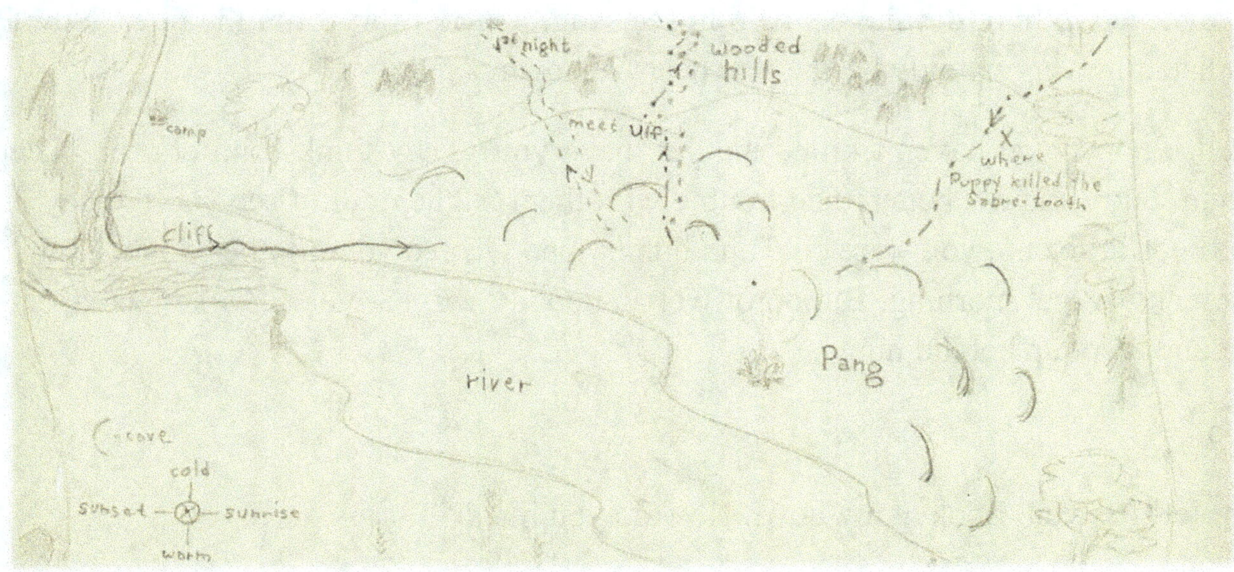

Chapter Three:
Fire's Plot

On one evening in late autumn after the fire, Dog was sitting in front of his cave, molding a large dish out of clay. While working, Dog talked to Puppy as he lay at his feet chewing a bone. It seemed nowadays Puppy and Jet were the only ones that ever listened to him, despite his help in securing their territory from the tiger. Now Puppy was listening very intently because he heard his own name.

"Well, Puppy, you haven't killed me yet, have you? They think I am crazy to keep you around, but we know better. The trouble with them is, they didn't see you the day I found you. Poor little cub, you were cold and hungry and wanted your mother. I had your mother for breakfast that morning. But don't worry, nobody will eat you." As he talked, Jet came over and crept up behind him.

"Boo!"

"Oh, Jet! It's you. Look at my bowl. How do you like it?"

Jet picked the bowl up and looked at it. It was much bigger than most of the bowls she had seen, and she wondered why he had made it so large. "It's for Puppy to eat from. I feed him so he won't want to hunt and run away from me." When Dog got the bowl patted into shape, he stuck it into the hot coals in a place where the logs made a sort of a natural oven. Then he went into the cave and soon came out with a piece of flint and a narrow shaft of wood.

"Making an arrow, Dog?" asked Jet.

"Maybe."

"For me?"

"Maybe." Dog turned his back to Jet and began chipping the flint for the arrowhead. Jet danced up and down behind him and begged him to tell her about it, but he would not.

"If you tell me, I will paint a design on Puppy's bowl."

"I guess you will do that anyhow. I won't tell you now. Later perhaps."

"All right for you. I won't listen later." Jet tossed her curls and disappeared into the cave.

Dog jumped up and called her. No answer. He called again. No answer. Picking up the flint and shaft, he ran into the cave calling, "Jet, don't be angry. I'll tell you."

The little glade in front of the cave was empty for several minutes, but then two evil-looking men stalked into the opening. One was painted with the juices of fruits and berries. He wore a huge headdress of fur and feathers, and his fur garment was covered with many tails, which bobbed up and down as he walked. He was Fire, the medicine man of the village. The other, Bok, was an ugly man with a scar on his face from the paw of a cave bear. His clothes were no different from any other cavemen, but the shape of his head and the way he walked showed him to be far inferior to Ulf or even to Fire. He was Fire's best friend because he would do anything Fire told him to do.

These two men stopped in front of Ulf's cave. Fire went over to the dozing Puppy and patted him on the head. Puppy rose, sniffed him, turned, and stalked into the cave. He wouldn't have anything to do with such people. Fire shrugged and walked over to Bok.

"You don't really believe he is crazy?" asked Bok in a low, stealthy tone.

"No," replied Fire, "I think taming the wolf was a good idea, and I mean to have Puppy for my own!"

"Well, take him," said Bok with a crafty smile, "You are the medicine man."

Fire stroked his chin. Usually, he could take what he wanted, but it seemed Puppy just wouldn't be taken. "I can't while Dog is alive," he said. "He won't leave Dog for some reason. I wonder how the boy tamed Puppy. He probably beats him."

Bok shook his head. "He says he is kind to the wolf."

"Kind? Bah! It's not true or good magic to tame by that method. You are wrong, Bok. But I am going to have Puppy for my own!" Fire pounded his fist into the palm of his other hand. There was a very sinister gleam in his eye. Bok was startled.

"You mean—"

"Yes, Bok, Dog must die!"

Bok bowed before Fire. "It shall be done."

The two men glanced about them and snuck off toward the main glade of the village. When they arrived there, Bok went into his cave and returned with a tom-tom. "Bok," said Fire, "today is the beginning of the Season of Little Game. We must appeal to the spirit of our tribe that we may have fortune in the hunt. Bok, call the people, and we will dance the dance of our fathers!"

Bok bowed deeply; and then went about the glade gathering sticks, dry autumn leaves, and moss. These he put into a pile in the middle of a circle of stones. There were the ashes of many such fires. He took a flint and stone, very much like the one Dog carried, and struck them together. "O Spirit of the fire," he called, "jump from your home in the flint and feed on these grasses I have provided. Grow! Light our dance that we may have good fortune!"

Many times, he hit the flint and stone together. Finally, a spark leapt forth and lit on the dry moss. A thin curl of smoke spiraled up, and soon a small orange flame crackled and jumped in the sticks and leaves. The ceremonial fire was lit.

Fire stood behind the flames with his arms upraised as Bok beat a slow tattoo on the tom-tom. Soon the glade began to fill with all the people of the village. Ulf, Sand, Jet, and Dog arrived at the same time as Jet's parents. They were not worried about their daughter because they knew she had been playing with the chief's son. They were surprised however, when they saw Jet making faces at Dog, who promptly made worse ones in response to her.

Fire stood behind the flames with his
arms upraised as Bok beat a slow
tattoo on the tom-tom.

When all the tribesmen were seated in a circle around Fire, he spoke in a loud, majestic voice. "Oh, spirit of the hunt, the Season of Little Game is now roaming the land! He has driven the fair season of plentiful food to far places. O spirit! Accept our dance and guide the feet of our hunters to the lairs of the wild beasts of the forest!"

Fire clapped, and the people formed a circle around him. Bok beat the tom-tom, slow at first, then faster and faster. It was night by that time, and the fire threw long shadows on the trees. Fire howled, and all the people echoed him. Bending, shaking, and jumping, the people danced around the circle. Then each man went over to a pile of torches, picked one up, and stuck the end into the fire as he danced. At the finish of the ceremony, each man waved his torch over his head and dropped from the circle. Soon Bok and Fire were alone again, though, in the distance, they could see the flicker of torches as the men lit the way for their families to go home.

During the days that followed, many parties of hunters went out and came back empty-handed. The people were beginning to murmur against Fire because his dance had brought no results. Dog wisely kept Puppy in the background, for when the dried meat ran out, the people might kill him and eat him. Dog was very troubled on that account and also because Jet was still angry with him.

Dog was also working on the arrow. The shaft was carved with beautiful saber tooth tigers, and there was a little blue feather in the end. Jet would surely be nice to him when she saw it. Still, she was very angry. Yesterday she had told him she didn't believe the story of the bear he had frightened. That bear–strange that the hunters had never brought back a bear from that region. Perhaps it was still there! Perhaps even if that bear wasn't there, another one might be!

"Father!" he called. "Father! Father!"

Ulf listened to Dog's idea but didn't know if he should send out hunters. He didn't believe Dog's story in the first place, but still, a berry patch might well have a bear den nearby.

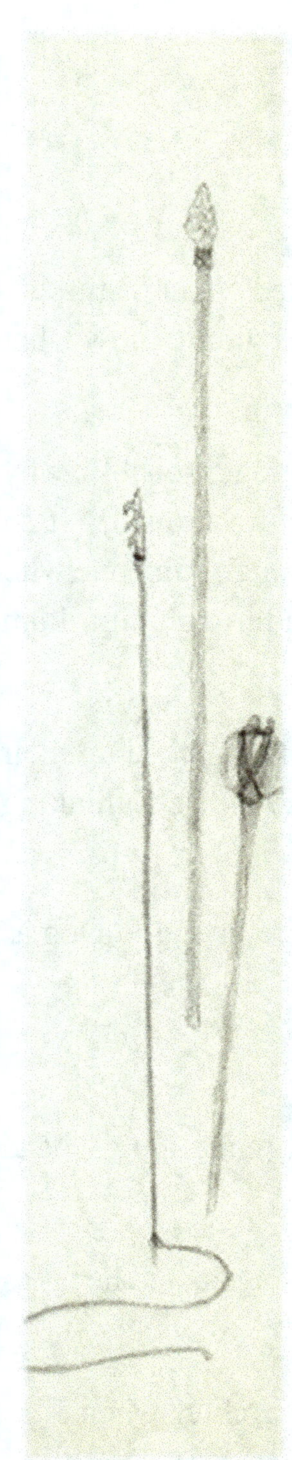

"All right, Dog, my hunters and I will go."

"I give you luck, Father."

"Luck? How could a crazy boy give luck? I will go now."

Dog went into the cave and sat down. He wasn't a crazy boy. He knew he wasn't. But still, maybe he was. Even Jet thought so now. She played with Tabat. Dog used to like him, but at the moment, he felt like sending the beautiful little arrow right into the other boy's heart. Instead, he hid the arrow in a crack in the wall above his bed. Ulf had carved a bison there, so its front hoof came right over the crack. The bison would protect the arrow. Dog crawled under the furs so his mother wouldn't see him and went to sleep.

The next day, Dog was startled by the joyful shouts of the returning hunters. They carried a huge old bear tied to a pole–probably the same one Dog had met several moons ago. He heard the women running out with flint knives to divide the bear amongst all of the families of Pang. *There would be food boiling tonight,* thought Dog. Peeking from the cave entrance, Dog saw Jet cutting a little piece of meat from the bear and eating it raw. He thought of the fun they used to have with a piece of meat. He would grab it from her, run, and eat some; then she would sneak up, grab it from him, and run. They kept this up until the meat was all gone. Now Tabat would probably play with her. But Jet ate her meat by herself, and then Dog shook his fist at Tabat for leaving Jet alone.

"Puppy, you still like me, don't you? Then, I don't care what the other people think." Dog and Puppy went back into the cave. They sat on the floor for several minutes.

A shadow fell across the entrance of the cave. It was a small shadow. Dog looked up, and Puppy jumped up and ran over to it.

"Jet!"

"Dog, do you want a piece of bear meat?"

"Jet, would you give me a piece?"

"Here it is. Show me the arrow, Dog."

While Dog and Jet were making peace, Ulf was talking to Fire, who seemed rather disturbed. "My son told me where to go find the bear. It is strange the medicine man didn't know what a crazy boy knew."

Fire stuttered. The other hunters were talking among themselves. Wondering, probably, why the medicine man couldn't guide them as well. "My brave hunters!" Fire droned, "It so happens that often the medicine man sends his messages to the people through someone who has the head sickness. Dog was close to you, Ulf, so I sent my message through him. I am finished."

Ulf and the hunters nodded. Fire's explanation sounded good enough. They picked up their spears, bows, and arrows and went toward their homes. Fire chuckled to himself, thinking how easily he explained his lack to the men.

Sand and Ulf started home together. They discussed the hunt and why Fire had used Dog as his message bearer.

"I wonder where Dog and Puppy are," said Sand.

"I don't care," Ulf answered. He was a little angry because Fire had made Dog's head sickness so plain to the other people. "I wish Dog would let us eat Puppy."

Sand disagreed, "I rather like Puppy. He growls when the other boys tease Dog, and he takes care of our little Sky so well."

"It's too bad our older son is different from other people. Who will be chief when I go hunting in the spirit world? And as for Puppy, I don't really want to eat him. Don't tell anyone though, or they will think we all have the head sickness." As Ulf spoke, he and Sand disappeared into the cave. They were surprised to find Jet and Dog painting Puppy's dish together. When the dish was finished and set to dry, Dog and Jet went outside. It was time for Jet to go home, and besides, she wanted to show her mother the arrow.

Before she had even disappeared, Dog's attention was taken by the sight of Fire limping toward him. His headgear was ripped apart, and his skin was all torn and bleeding.

"Ho, Dog!" he called with a forced smile. "Tell me, how do you catch hold of your wolf long enough to beat him until he is tame?"

"I don't beat him. I am kind to him. That is the way to make an animal tame."

"Bah!" said Fire.

"I hope those marks from teeth and claws heal soon," remarked Dog.

"Bah!" Fire responded, and he limped away as Dog laughed. Dog knew Fire had tried to catch and tame a full-grown wolf, and now the wolf was gone, and it was a wonder Fire wasn't gone, too! Dog whistled to Puppy, and the two went out into the woods to see if they could find some nuts.

Fire turned just in time to see Dog and Puppy disappear. He grabbed a stout club, called Bok, and ran toward the boy and wolf. The time had come for him to do away with Dog and make Puppy his own!

Several minutes later, Sand came out of the cave and called her son. When he didn't answer, she assumed he was playing in the woods with Jet. *Maybe they were hunting for some more wolf cubs.* She turned to go into the cave, when suddenly, she heard a great commotion from the forest. Ulf rushed out and demanded to know what the noise was that woke him up so rudely.

"Oh! Oh! Oh! Maybe Puppy did turn on Dog! Oh, my poor boy! How foolish we were to keep the wolf!"

Ulf put his arm around her. "Don't worry," he said. "Dog has his knife, so maybe he will kill the wolf. Perhaps the wolf is the demon who has his mind, and when he kills it, the head sickness will leave him."

"But Dog is only a little boy. How could he kill a wolf? Ulf! Look!"

Sand pointed to the edge of the forest. Fire, his ceremonial regalia quite battered, and Bok, who was very scared, burst from the woods and ran past Ulf and Sand right through the village with Puppy close on their heels! Puppy was all wolf, snarling and angry. No wonder the medicine man and his friend were afraid! A minute later, Dog came running up to them. He was panting and excited but unhurt.

"Oh, Mother! Listen!" he exclaimed between breaths. "They tried to kill me, and my wolf isn't a wolf any more, and he chased them, and I was scared, but Puppy wasn't!"

Ulf took Dog by the shoulders and shook him. "Tell your story to me straight."

"Fire and Bok! They tried to kill me, but Puppy chased them out of the village! He wouldn't let them hurt me, see? I told you my wolf isn't a wolf anymore!"

When he heard this recital, Ulf whistled long in surprise. *Strange that the medicine man should be afraid of anything. And how odd Fire had acted the day I caught the bear!*

Ulf's thoughts were interrupted by Sand. "I am so glad that you are alive! Puppy is a hero. The spirit of our people must have given you great magic, so you could tame the wolf and make him serve you, Dog."

Sand's words convinced Ulf that Dog had been thinking right. "Yes," he said, "Dog has done something for our tribe. What has Fire ever done? Perhaps Puppy chased Fire because he was not the real medicine man. I will take it up with the tribe."

The three walked over to the council circle. Dog found the tom-tom in Bok's vacant cave. Ulf pounded the message, and soon all the people were gathering to hear the chief's words. They had seen the race through the village, and they now saw the very tired Puppy returning to lie down at the feet of Dog. The people knew Ulf's message would explain these strange happenings, so they hurried, and soon the glade was full. Ulf raised his arms.

"I, chief of Pang, call you to relate how your high priest of the fire was driven away! He tried to kill my son, whom you call crazy!"

The people were astonished and murmured among themselves. These happenings were very strange. Even Bearclaw, who was the oldest man in the village, could not think of anything so odd.

"The wolf," Ulf continued, "whom my son made love him, stopped this act and drove the medicine man away! We now have no medicine man, but it is well, for he was a wicked man, and probably the cause of the fire eating our village during the Season of Dry Grasses!"

This was a new idea to the people, but after talking it over amongst themselves, they decided Ulf was right. Ulf was a good chief and usually right. Ulf raised his hand again. "And now I say, let my son, who is not crazy but very wise, be our new medicine man!"

By this time, the people were very excited, and they shouted gladly, "Yes! Yes! Dog, the boy medicine man! Good! Good!"

Ulf called out again. "The headgear!"

One of the men brought Fire's badly damaged headgear from the place where it had fallen as he ran away. Ulf took it and held it over Dog's head. "I, the chief, make you high medicine man. You must work for your tribe, hunt, and be a great warrior as well, so that the spirit of the fire will be pleased!" Amidst the cheering of the crowd, Ulf placed the headgear on Dog. Then he went on. "I have more to say. As Dog has tamed the great wolf, I say he has changed the wolf into a different animal! Shall we call the new wolf by the name of my son, the dog?"

"Yes! Yes! The dog!" yelled the people almost at once. When they finally quieted, Dog arose.

"Now that I am medicine man, I want to make a new rule. All the people of Pang shall be kind to Puppy, and all shall have wolf cubs to turn into dogs. Because we love these dogs, they shall protect us from saber-toothed tigers and other wild animals and make unfriendly tribes afraid to come and rob us!"

"The boy speaks wisdom," nodded old Bearclaw, and the people loudly took up the cry. "Someday," said Bearclaw, "every boy in the world will have a dog protector."

Dog seemed worried, but when he heard Bearclaw speak, his face cleared. "Listen," he voiced, "I am only a boy and not yet old enough nor wise enough to be a medicine man. First, I must learn to hunt, fight, and be a man. There is someone here much better fitted to wear the headgear than I. Old Bearclaw, come here." Dog made the surprised old man the new medicine man and also made him his firm friend. Bearclaw had always wanted that honor, and Dog would rather be just an ordinary little boy and hunt, fish, and play with Jet for the time being. Now was not his time to be medicine man, someone who was always burdened with the dignity of that great towering hat.

"Now go," said Bearclaw, "and every time you kill a wolf, be sure to bring home her cubs."

"Hail the new medicine man, and Ulf, our mighty chief!" yelled the people, and they danced around, howling gleefully for several minutes before they gradually began to go home. Soon Sand, Ulf, Jet, Dog, and Puppy were the only ones left.

"I'm proud of you, son," said Ulf. "You were wise to give the honor to an old man, and I am glad."

"I knew your kindness to Puppy would repay you," exclaimed Sand, and she and Ulf went off to their cave.

Jet smiled proudly and patted Puppy on the head. "Well, Puppy, I guess we all showed them."

"We!" hooted Dog. "Puppy and I did. Isn't that just like a girl?"

"Woof!" said Puppy.

Chapter Four:

Two Not-So-Brave Hunters

After Fire and Bok had been driven away from the village, Dog was amazed at his own popularity. All his old friends, and many new ones, flocked around him and tried to warm up to Puppy. Ulf and Sand knew many of these children would forget him soon, but Dog decided he must be a hero, and his position was everlasting. He played with the boys, and when Jet wanted to go along, he airily told her to go learn to cook with the rest of the girls. Great hunters had no time for such things. Tabat was his special pal. These two had been like brothers for many years when they were younger, and Sand was glad to see he did not give up his old friend. Tabat was very proud of being Dog's partner and soon began to think that he, too, was a hero. The result was two little boys who thought they were overly important.

One day Jet came up to him. "Dog, don't you like me anymore?"

"Of course, I like you, Jet, only you're a girl, and we men have no time for girls."

"Let me go hunting with you just this once."

"No. Tabat and Puppy and I are going alone. We can't be bothered with girls or those other boys, even."

"This is a funny time to go hunting. The morning the ground was white and hard. That means the animals will be all gone. Pretty soon will be dried meat time, and you think you can find good hunting. You are silly."

"Don't worry, we will bring home meat," boasted Dog.

"I suppose you think you are a better hunter than Ulf. He stays home now."

"Well, no, but nearly as good."

"I don't believe I like you so well anymore, Dog. You think you are too good."

"Oh, what does a girl's opinion mean anyhow? You don't know a thing about such matters." With that snappy speech, Dog was off to find Tabat. Puppy followed him happily. He had heard the word 'hunt' and knew a trip into the woods was in store.

Even though they thought they were the bravest boys in the world, each could not resist taking some dried meat in his pouch just to be on the safe side. The morning was bright, and the sun warmed the frostbitten earth, but the sharp tang of winter was with them all day. They cut up through the hills because it was shorter, and they wouldn't have to cross the narrow gorge. They decided to go back up to the old village and camp one night in a deserted cave. So, after they got into the hills, they headed for the stream.

"It's cold, Dog. Let's make some feet-skins as soon as we kill an animal," suggested Tabat.

"Ho! You are too soft, Tabat. Look at my feet. They are hard!"

Dog held his foot up so Tabat could see the calloused bottoms. Tabat saw, but he saw something else, too.

"Maybe they have thick skin, but they are blue. You are just as cold as I am, Dog."

"Well, don't admit it!" snapped Dog. All day they had not even seen an animal, and Jet's words were beginning to come back very strongly to him. As evening came, they realized that it wasn't just their feet that were cold. Dog remembered Sand wanting him to wrap his feet in a pair of small pelts, but he had said no--he was tough, and he could make some himself if he got cold.

They found a sheltered place between a rock and a fallen tree. There they built a fire and slept off their hunger. They reasoned that hunting would surely be better tomorrow.

The next morning, they each ate a piece of the dried meat and some nuts which grew nearby. Except where their fire had been burning, the ground was whitened with a heavy frost. They jumped up and down to loosen their stiff muscles. They were uncomfortable but not in any danger. The boys were used to hardships, and this wasn't much worse than many they had endured. The sad thing about this was the foolhardiness of it. Perhaps the mighty men weren't quite so mighty!

While the boys were warming themselves, Puppy ran around in circles barking and then stopped to hear the clear, sharp echo. He liked that echo. He barked once, cocked his ear, and listened. It was a mystifying sound but very pleasant.

"Listen," said Tabat. "The spirit of the hills is answering Puppy. Hear how near it is!"

"Yes. And the sun mammoth is high. Come on, or we will never get to the old village."

"I hate to put out this fire."

"You must." The dirt was frozen hard, and they could not bury the fire, so Dog took a big stick and snuffed out the flames. When it was completely out, the two boys and the wolf started again. Dog's toes felt that if he hit them, they would break off with a loud crack. How he wished for his mother's feet-skins!

They were going at a pretty good pace when Tabat noticed Puppy was limping. He had cut his paw on a sharp piece of ice that had formed in a puddle. Dog washed the cut with water from the chilly stream. Puppy whimpered and licked Dog's ear. When they started again, he walked on three legs and felt very sorry for himself.

In the early afternoon, a small burrowing animal scampered across the path. Tabat quickly aimed his bow and arrow, and although he didn't kill it, he pinned it to the ground by the tail. Small work was needed to finish it and build a fire. It made only a mouthful for each, but it was fresh meat and had a pelt!

"Who gets it?" asked Tabat. Dog pointed to Puppy, who lay by the fire licking his hurt foot.

"He does. We will make a foot-skin for him. Besides, it is too small for either of us. Come here, Puppy." Dog wrapped Puppy's foot and tied it around the ankle with a piece of intestine. Puppy seemed pleased and was able to walk on it after a few tries. Dog and Tabat, still barefooted but feeling much better, prepared to continue on the trail. By nightfall, they planned to be at the den where Dog found Puppy.

"Tabat! Come here!" Dog called excitedly. He had gone a little way ahead and was studying the trail intently. Tabat ran up to him.

"What did you find, Dog?"

"A footprint, frozen in the ground! See? It is large and flat, not like ours." Dog got on his hands and knees to study it better.

"It looks like the footprint of Bok or of Fire's wife. They are different from the rest of the tribe."

"Bok? Oh, no. Bok is dead, I am sure. It's leading up the trail. Come on, here's another–and another! Let's follow them!" The boys and Puppy crept silently up the trail. They were careful as they realized that even a footprint might mean the presence of an enemy.

Dog got on his hands and knees to
study it better.

All the rest of the day, they followed the strange trail. It was nearly dark when they came to a little den. It looked as though it had not been entered since the night Dog and Puppy decided they should be friends. Now Puppy sniffed around the den in the dead leaves. Far back in his mind was the memory of a furry mother and of cold and hunger, until the little boy came and carried him home. It was Puppy's first contact with his old life and the wolf ways of his kind. Yet, when he saw the warm fire, he was not afraid, as are other wolves. The very faint scents of the cave were not enough to draw him back. He had learned that fire was good if he did not touch it, and the piece of dried meat Dog tossed to him was much more sure than the possibility of tracking down a larger game on his own.

That night they finished the meat they had with them. They would have to find food tomorrow, but they were confident, and that night large pieces of cooked meat floated in front of them in their dreams. Surely this was an omen of good luck!

The next day they followed the old trail by the stream. The footprints were still there and were very deep. They had probably been made during the rain and then frozen.

When the boys reached the pond, Dog showed Tabat how to catch fish. Sand had taught Dog, as her native village was located near a tribe that belonged to a race of fishermen. Sand had learned to eat fish there, and she passed her knowledge on to Ulf and Dog. Tabat didn't like this strange new food very well, but he was so hungry he ate it anyhow. The two boys had three fish apiece, and then they fixed some for Puppy.

It was surprising what a full stomach could do for a boy. The two felt at peace as they sat by the fire. They knew they would find a reindeer or bison and bring it home victorious. Even Puppy decided his foot wasn't so painful, and he stopped licking the bandage and went to sleep.

"Look at the short little log, Tabat. It looks as though a jab with my spear would send it rolling." Dog pushed the log. As he shoved, he accidentally let go of the spear. The motion of the log carried the spear away with it until the little weapon fell off.

"Look, Tabat, how the log took my spear and carried it!" Dog was astonished. He had never noticed such a thing before.

"If it carried your spear, why wouldn't it carry a bundle if we could fix it so it wouldn't fall off?" asked Tabat. He was lazy and hated to carry bundles, almost worse than he hated to run.

They brought the log back and set a stone on it. Again, they shoved; it carried the stone for a short way, and then threw it off. Then they dragged the log to the top of the little slope, and this time, Dog emptied his pouch and set it on the top. Tabat put an arrow into the pouch to hold it. They set the log rolling over the pouch and arrow, and the arrow was crushed by the weight of the log. That method surely would never work!

"It seems to me," said Dog, "that there must be a way to make a rolling log carry bundles. When we get back home, let's try some more." Tabat agreed, and they took to the trail again.

Dog stopped and stared. It was evening, and they were in the glade of the old village. "Look, Tabat, isn't that a woman?" Tabat's gaze followed Dog's finger. It certainly was a woman of the same coarse type as Fire's wife. Then they saw other people around. *Some tribe had moved into the barren old village! They must have needed homes very desperately.*

"So!" boomed a voice behind them. "What luck!" The boys whirled and faced–Fire! He was grinning with pleasure at the kind fate which brought to him, unprotected, the son of his worst enemy. "Where is your great tame wolf? Did he run away from you?"

Dog and Tabat looked around. Puppy was indeed gone! He had not even entered the glade with them! "He–he was here a short time ago," stuttered Dog. Fire laughed. Dog had never heard such a loud or horrid laugh. It made him shiver even worse than the cold.

Fire took each boy by the shoulder and walked them up to what had been his old cave. It was now occupied by a short heavy woman who looked very strangely at the two boys.

"The Great Spirit of the tribe of Fire has sent these boys to be sacrificed to him. I give them to your keeping. Do not let them get away!"

Dog and Tabat looked at each other. *Sacrificed?* That meant they would be killed! Fire pushed them roughly into the cave. The woman said nothing.

From the entrance of the cave, Dog could see Fire and his old friend, Bok, sitting in the glade with their heads together. They were discussing this very important ceremony. Dog noticed the woman was watching them as well. He was in the back of her. It was a long chance, but he'd try it. If he made it, Tabat could follow.

It was a long chance, but he'd try it.

He crept silently out of the cave. As long as the woman looked the other way, he was safe. The woman whirled and whipped out a long sinew with a rock tied to the end. Expertly, she tossed the rock, and it spun around Dog's neck, jerking him off balance. She pulled him to her, cuffed his ears, and pushed him back into the cave. Still, she never spoke a word.

Now Dog and Tabat were thoroughly frightened. They crept into the darkest corner of the cave and sat there in wait. The cave was cold. The little fire at the entrance didn't throw any heat back to where the boys huddled. The woman squatted behind it and blocked any warmth that might creep in. Her shadow fell across the cave floor, and it moved around with the dancing of the flames. When she threw a stick of wood on the fire, the shadow would shoot out and cover part of the wall as well as the floor. As the fire died, the shadow shortened until the strange, silent woman put on more fuel. Many times during the night, the shadow rose and fell, and neither the boys nor the woman slept. Toward morning a fog rolled in, and by the time it was daylight rose, the sun was only a pale-yellow speck in the sky.

"No-Tongue! No-Tongue!" a voice called. It sounded far away, and the boys could see no one. The woman rose and raised her hand. Suddenly, Bok stepped into the circle of the fire. The boys had not seen him coming through the thick fog, and this sudden appearance appeared magical! "No-Tongue, are the boys here?" he asked.

No-Tongue nodded and pointed to their corner. Bok peered in and smiled. "Good. Feed them." He then disappeared into the mist.

No-Tongue came into the cave and cut two large pieces of meat from a reindeer carcass that hung on the wall. She tossed them to the boys. Then she cut another piece and ate it as she squatted by the fire. The meat wasn't particularly fresh, but the cold weather had preserved it somewhat. It was very good for Dog and Tabat because they were very hungry.

Several hours later, the boys heard many voices in the fog. The voices were yelling and singing. The sacrifice would begin soon.

"We must be brave and not cry," whispered Dog, and Tabat nodded. The fog was lifting a little, and they could see the shapes of the people as they danced around a great central fire. No-Tongue beckoned to the boys, and they joined the crowd. No-Tongue pushed the boys into the middle of the circle. The people shouted at them, and from the confused jumble of words, Dog and Tabat learned that they were to be eaten! They had never heard of eating human beings before. It just couldn't be true, but it was! Last night's dream of cooked meat came back to their minds. Instead of being an omen of good luck, it was just the opposite! Dog closed his eyes so he wouldn't see the cannibals. Tabat couldn't close his. It seemed he just had to look, even though it frightened him. Fire and Bok had not yet arrived, and Dog wished they would hurry and get it over with.

Suddenly the singing changed to shrieks of terror as the people shrank back to admit something or someone into the inner circle.

"Puppy!" yelled Tabat, and Dog opened his eyes. It didn't seem possible–yet there was Puppy, followed by another wolf, who was only half-grown! Puppy jumped on Dog while barking, whining, and wagging his tail! He had run away from his master and now begged forgiveness. The other wolf was afraid and huddled close to Puppy. She was thin, cold, and hungry. Perhaps if she had been well-fed, she would never have followed the big Puppy so close to a human or a fire. Now she was too terrified to be wild, and when Tabat picked her up, she just whimpered and snuggled close to him for warmth.

"Look," murmured the people, "these boys must have great magic! Even the wolves bow down to them!" They, too, bowed deeply to the two surprised boys. Dog sensed the situation and raised his hand.

"We are displeased. We came to be friendly, but you captured us. We go now. Bring feet-skins!"

A couple of trembling women left and returned with four pelts and some sinew. Another brought a bundle of dried meat and gave it to Dog.

The boys tied on the feet-skins and walked out of the glade with their noses in the air. As soon as they reached the charred forest, they ran as fast as they could. Fire and Bok would be returning soon and would chase them. Tabat was still carrying the other wolf. Puppy tugged Dog's foot-skin and ran to one side. He returned and looked at the boys. Then he ran again. Dog and Tabat caught the idea and followed. Soon they reached a den that was hidden behind a tall growth of grass. It had been out of the path of the great fire. Here,

Puppy had found the little wolf. They crawled into the den, and Dog straightened the tangle of grass and vines from the inside. It looked quite undisturbed.

Back in the village, Fire and Bok ran into the circle of cowering people.

"Dance!" roared Fire. "Bring in the boys! No-Tongue, have you left them alone? Run and fetch them before they escape!"

One of the men came forward. "We make mistake. Boys had great magic. Two wolves came. Did them homage!"

"You let them go?" shrieked Bok.

"They were angry. They demanded feet-skins before they go. And meat!"

"Hyenas!" howled Fire. "Your heads are the heads of dumb beasts! Those boys weren't magic. Of all the wolves in the world, those two are the only tame ones! Come, witless ones, we must find them!"

The men gathered their weapons and set out behind Fire and Bok. They followed the same general direction taken by the boys.

There was scarcely a sound inside the little den. Even the animals seemed to sense the need for quiet. Dog opened the package of meat and gave a lot of it to Puppy and his friend. He figured much food would make them sleepy, and there would be less danger of noise. He and Tabat ate sparingly to save on the rations.

"See how she tears at the meat," said Dog. "I shall call her Knife Tooth."

Dog figured right. This was the finest meal she had eaten ever since she could remember. The wildness went out of her, and she went to sleep beside her great protector, Puppy.

Puppy heard them first. He sat up with his ears up and his head cocked to one side. He growled deep down in his throat. Dog told him to be quiet, and they all listened. Soon, they heard Fire's voice saying he thought the boys weren't far away. They pressed against the back wall of the den. What if the men should notice the entrance?

"Come, men without brains," they heard Fire say, "where would they naturally go?"

"Toward the stream," answered a man's voice.

"Then they probably went toward the sunrise, as they have more brains than you. We go inland." Fire's voice faded as he and his men filed past the hidden den. Dog and Tabat started immediately toward the stream. This time, Tabat carried the meat, and Dog carried Knife Tooth. The frozen ground didn't hurt their feet now, and they ran swiftly toward the other wolf den. It was nearly evening, and they had to hurry to get there before dark. They stumbled through the underbrush and toward the sunset. They knew they could find the stream in that direction.

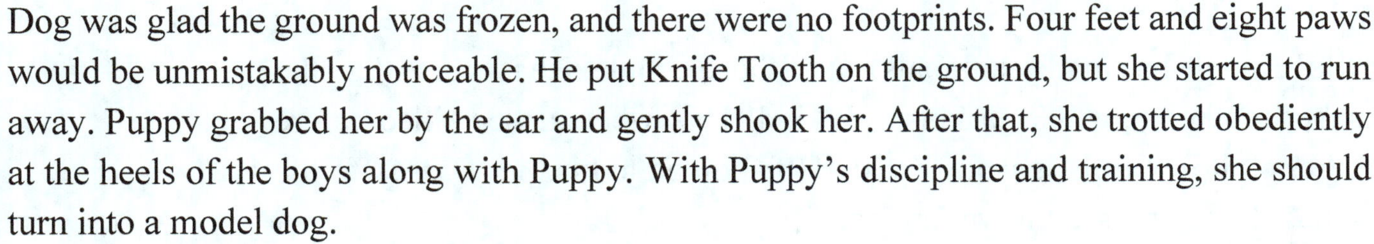

Tabat had never traveled so fast before. He was panting heavily as he did his best to keep up with Dog and Puppy. He didn't complain because he knew Fire might decide to turn back at any time, and maybe he already had, so Tabat raced on with his friend. He had less desire to be eaten than to run.

The fog had lifted, and the night was a clear one. Dog decided they should keep going, so they would reach home the following evening. All thoughts of sleep were impossible; therefore, Tabat agreed that it might be better to put as much distance as they could between themselves and Fire.

Dog was glad the ground was frozen, and there were no footprints. Four feet and eight paws would be unmistakably noticeable. He put Knife Tooth on the ground, but she started to run away. Puppy grabbed her by the ear and gently shook her. After that, she trotted obediently at the heels of the boys along with Puppy. With Puppy's discipline and training, she should turn into a model dog.

The moon was kind to the four. It shone big and silver and lit the way. It sent white sparkles to the stream and frost to frighten the demons that prowled in the night. Each step between themselves and Fire made the boys more confident. Downstream, they trotted, and almost before they knew it, they were at the spot where they cut inland to cross the hills. Soon after that, they were at the place where they had spent the first night. They decided to sleep there for the few hours remaining until dawn.

Fire and his men searched all day but found nothing inland. He was furious and raged at his followers for allowing themselves to be fooled by two small boys. "Tomorrow," he yelled, "we go down the stream!"

But tomorrow found the boys inland as they crossed the hills. They had finished the meat and felt much encouraged by the course of events. They walked fast, because of all the places in the world, these wonderful hunters wanted only their own caves.

Dog stopped. He put one finger to his lips and listened. "I hear footsteps–hide!" he whispered, and the boys jumped behind a fallen tree, quickly followed by Puppy and Knife Tooth. The footsteps came closer. It was a party of men, and they seemed very happy. The boys could hear low voices talking and laughing. Dog peeked over the log as the leader came over the top of the little hill. It was Ulf! Dog and Tabat raced toward the group and called to them. Ulf turned and shouted for his men to come up.

"Where is your game?" he asked.

"We didn't get any," said Dog. "Fire captured us and was going to eat us, but Puppy saved us. This is Knife Tooth. Puppy found her in the forest!"

Ulf had heard only one word. "Fire? I thought Fire was dead."

"No, Father. He is chief of a tribe of Bok's people up in our old village! He hates you!"

"So! And he has made cannibals out of those people. He is worse than the saber-toothed tiger. He eats his own kind! This tribe must be killed before others follow Fire's terrible ideas!" Ulf shouted to his men, "Back to the village! We prepare for war at once!"

Dog and Tabat looked at each other. This was great excitement, and they wished they were big enough to go with the hunters. The little party went back to the village. When they arrived, the tribe of Pang wondered

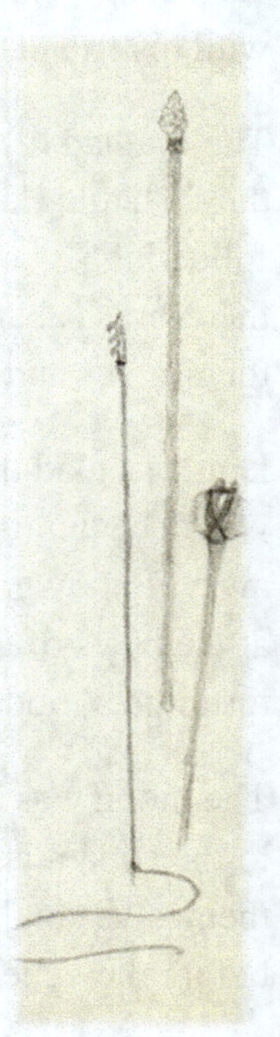

mightily what made them return so soon with such determined looks on their faces.

Each man went to his own cave. Sand saw Ulf, Dog, Puppy, and Knife Tooth coming and knew something terrible had happened. Dog explained the entire story as they ate, and Sand grew frightened. She hated the thought of Ulf going away and killing people.

"Ulf, don't go!" Sand urged. "Those people are far away and can't hurt us! Please stay!"

Ulf shook his head. Eating humans was wrong, and he felt he had to put a stop to it. Killing was the only way he knew how to accomplish this goal. So, around the council fire that night, he shouted for war, and the people danced for many hours. But Sand knew they wouldn't dance tomorrow!

Chapter Five:

The Battle

"But Ulf!" exclaimed Sand, "Surely not the little boys!"

"Yes, Sand. I have been thinking for a long time. The boys will be safe. They will take bows and arrows and go up in the trees. When we attack, they will be hidden and will shoot from above."

"You are very wise. Are you going to take Puppy and Knife Tooth? They could kill many."

"No. Even though they are changed to dogs, still, killing human beings might turn them back into wolves again. I thought that out, too, and decided I am right."

"Of course you are." Sand turned to attend to little Sky, who was crying. She smiled. It was nice that Ulf was the wisest man in the village. As wise as the first great chieftain, old Pang, she felt sure.

Dog was very excited. He got his bow and all of his arrows together and joined a gathering of boys.

"Dog," called a voice, and Dog turned to see Jet, standing by a tree on the river's edge. He ran over to her.

"Hello, Jet. I am glad I saw you before we left."

"I've got something for you." She held out her hand. In it was the pretty little arrow with the blue feather. "I want you to take it so you will have another arrow. I don't want you to get killed, Dog."

Dog took the arrow. He felt very strange, almost as if he were going to cry. Instead, he smiled. "You are a kind girl, Jet. Don't worry, I'll be back." After that, he turned and walked toward the boys. He stuck the arrow into his fur quiver, and the group fell in behind the party of men. They were on the march at last!

Ulf decided to go the whole distance inland, as it was shorter and also the least-used route. Fire would expect a war party to come up the stream. The other path had no water nearby. Fire reckoned without the wisdom of Ulf, who fashioned bags of skin for each man to carry his own water. They were a well-supplied and well-directed army of mighty fighters. If the other tribe were not too many, they should win, but Ulf was afraid of the odds. His own band was small, and Dog had seen what seemed like countless numbers of Fire's people. That was the reason for putting the boys in the trees—it would swell Ulf's army very much.

The overland trail cut a whole day from the march. Soon they were hidden just outside of the old glade. Ulf gathered his men around him for instruction. "Boys, get up into the trees and aim mostly at those who are about to kill any of our men. Up now!" He waited until they were safely installed and hidden in the branches of the trees that still were covered with leaves. This section had been left by the great fire. He continued, "We will surround the glade and some of us will get into sight and start howling at them. When they attack, we will draw the battle out here under the trees, and that's where you and the boys come in." The men nodded. Their chief was indeed wise beyond his years, for his beard was still soft and scarcely longer than that of a young man.

Ulf and a small group went into the glade. "Where is Fire, the coward?" They shouted. "Where is his tribe of field mice? Eaters of human beings, you are lower than the mangy hyenas!"

Ulf saw people peering at him from their caves. Then he saw Bok, who looked surprised and disappeared. A moment later, Fire came roaring from his cave.

"It is Ulf! He plans to kill you as you sleep! Come and fight and show him you are not cowards!" Fire's great voice drove the people into an angry mood. The sight of Ulf and only a few others alone gave them courage. They rushed them with weapons.

Ulf and his men retreated slowly. Great-Tooth and One-Eye were killed in the first rush, but not before two of the stocky tribe were accounted for. The others came out of hiding, and the great hand-to-hand battle started. They used knives and spears, but mostly, they used great stone axes. One well-aimed blow with the stone axe could split a man's skull, and he would sink to the ground for another man to stumble over without even a howl!

Dog watched, fascinated. He almost forgot his part in the fight until he saw a man behind Ulf with his great club upraised. Twang–he shot—and the man fell howling with an arrow in his throat!

Fire was brave in battle. He raged back and forth, shouting courage into the hearts of his inferior followers. They needed it. The huge size of the men of Pang and the arrows that seemed to come from nowhere terrified them. Ulf longed for an encounter with Fire, but he was always too heavily beset to challenge the former witch-doctor. As for Fire himself, he seemed to be trying to keep out of Ulf's way.

Dog watched, fascinated.

One from the stocky tribe glanced upward and saw a small foot dangling from a branch. "Archers in trees!" he yelled. "They are only boys!" He started up that very tree. Tabat was up that tree and took careful aim. The man tottered backward and crashed. The same thing happened to any other who dared climb into each boy's domain.

"Leave them alone!" shouted Fire. "They will soon run out of death sticks." He cursed the minds of his warriors, who had not been able to grasp the idea of the bow and arrow. Fire was right–young Fox Ear did run out of arrows, but he was an intelligent lad. Fire was astonished to see a stick, with the end whittled to a deadly point, pierce a fighter's eye!

It was then Fire knew his cause was lost. How could he, even with greater numbers, ever hope to crush such people? How foolish he had been to try to make warriors out of this race! By nature, they had been a peaceful, roaming sort of herdsmen. He sought to make them fierce by feeding them human flesh, and now he knew he had failed, just as he had failed to make them give up their herds of reindeer and become hunters. Fire was distraught.

The men were soon without the huge booming voice that had urged them to fury. Ulf could no longer find the tall, insolent figure of the man he sought to kill. The battle waned. Then the tribe of Fire threw down their arms and fled, panic-stricken. Without their leader, fear crept into their minds, and they ran–just as Fire himself had done, though nobody had seen him go.

Ulf gave the signal to stop fighting, and moving to the head of his men, of whom comparatively few were dead, he strode into the open glade.

"Come out," he called. "We have left our arms behind. I want to talk to you!" He raised both hands in the signal for peace. Slowly from the caves came what was left of the stocky herdsmen. Ulf spoke again. "Who was your leader before Fire came?" They pointed to one of the men, who rose. "What did your people do?" asked Ulf.

The man answered, "I am Dar. These are my people. We love peace and tend reindeer. Reindeer make us food and clothing, so we have no need to hunt or kill. Fire came. He told us to eat people, hunt, and be fierce, but he is gone now. What do we do?”

“Where did you come from, and where are your herds?” questioned Ulf.

“From the cold lands. We find this village and live here. Our herds are in hills up there.” He pointed toward the north. “Fire would not let us tend our herds, and our animals scattered.”

Ulf smiled. “Send out a party of men to round up your reindeer. Live here in peace. When it is winter and our food is scarce, we will bring long-haired pelts and knives to trade for reindeer meat. Good?”

“Good,” answered Dar, and the two men put their hands on each other’s shoulders to seal the bargain. Dar ordered food and a ceremonial dance around the fire

The women brought out two large, forked branches cut from a tree. Each of these was placed by a woman on either side of the fire. Several more women brought out a large reindeer carcass spitted onto a long slender pole. They laid the pole across the two forks so the reindeer was directly in the flames. A good feast was in store for the weary fighters.

As soon as the outside of the deer was roasted, the women cut off slices and tossed them to the men, who squatted by the fire. Dog sat next to Ulf and was very proud that he was Ulf’s son. He knew the other boys wished their fathers were chief, but Dog didn’t feel conceited; he only felt he would have to work hard to be such a good chief. He chewed slowly on his piece of meat as he visualized himself leading a band of men into a fight and winning as well as Ulf had. Ulf, however, was not entirely satisfied—the one man he had wanted to get had escaped. Bok was thoroughly subdued and had promised to stay with his own people and stir up no more trouble. It was Fire Ulf wanted to know about.

When Fire deserted the battle, he headed northward to the place where the herdsmen had left their animals. There, close to a spring, he dug himself a cave. As long as the reindeer were kept there, he would have no trouble finding food, and there was water close by. Fire decided to live in this place and bide his time until he could show his face to the other men. Here he would stay until circumstances brought him and Ulf face to face again, and then Ulf would surely die! Fire gloated over his plan as he thought of how he would get revenge on his enemy. The next day he started toward Pang. He would creep in during the night and fetch his wife and children. He craved company in the wilderness.

Ulf and his men decided to stay in the village of the Reindeer clan, as it was called, all night. The roasted reindeer was only a skeleton, and the fire burned low when the feast broke up. Each man wanted to stay with the family that occupied his old cave.

They found a very young couple and a very old woman in Ulf's old place. Ulf showed them the secret of the indoor fire. At first, they were afraid of it, and the old woman screeched that it was bad magic until Ulf told them he had one all the time in the new cave, and it was only good. However, the old woman wasn't convinced until the fire began to warm her bed in the back of the cave. Soon she was clucking with contentment and calling Ulf 'My son.'

Dog liked these people now. No-Tongue had given him the rock and thong she used to catch him that day, which seemed so long ago. The young man named Lob gave Dog a fine reindeer head with long, branched antlers. Ulf had received something he thought was far

better than gifts. He had made peace between the two tribes and felt very happy. Tomorrow he could go back to Sand and tell her that all is well. Yes, the venture to the north had been a success!

In the morning, Pang's men joined the others in digging a shallow hole. In this, they placed the bodies of all the dead with their weapons beside them. After covering them with earth, they built a big stone cairn over the whole common grave. The men worked hard, and when it was finished, the Reindeer medicine man arose.

"The bodies of these men here, they are alive in the spirit world. They have met their fathers and are hunting in land of plenty game. They are all together now. They have peace. We have peace, too." The people nodded. The women whose husbands had been killed were all together on one side of the cairn. They wailed, howled, and threw themselves on the ground. The medicine man spoke to them. "Get up. Your husbands come back in sleep adventures. You will see your husbands again. Go back to your caves and children." The women withdrew, and soon the cairn was deserted. The Reindeer people went back to their daily tasks, and Ulf and his men started homeward.

Ulf didn't have his giant bow and arrow with him because he had wanted the boys to do the shooting in the fight. He was unprepared when Dog saw the reindeer. The two were in the lead, and as they skirted a small hill, Dog saw the animals grazing under an oak tree. He put his finger to his lips and pointed.

Ulf took Dog's bow, which really wasn't small, and motioned for Fern, the father of Tabat, to come forward with his son's weapon. The two men bent the bows back until they nearly split. "Sst," said Ulf softly, and at the signal, the two arrows flew toward their marks. The doe fell without a sound, but the buck roared and shook his antlers at the men. He charged straight toward Tabat, who started to run, but he tripped and fell instead.

Fern fitted an arrow to his bow, but he was trembling so much that the death stick didn't reach its true mark. It hit the reindeer in the flank instead of the heart. However, the shot did accomplish something. It turned the beast's attention from poor Tabat to his father. Bellowing with rage, the buck wheeled and charged again.

Fern was brave. He did not run. Now that his son was out of danger, he was very calm. He fitted another arrow to the bow and took careful aim. As the beast came rushing toward him, he let go. The arrow hit the buck head-on, right between its eyes. Fern didn't even look at the fallen reindeer but ran over to Tabat, who was still sitting on the ground.

"Are you all right? Get up. See, I have killed the reindeer, so you can have some antlers like Dog's."

Tabat nodded. He was still too scared to speak. Then he rose and laughed. It was all over now, but he felt sure he had been on the ground for several seasons.

The men trussed up the animals and started again. Such incidents meant nothing to them. They happened all the time. The party sang boisterously as it neared the village of Pang.

Perhaps they would not have been so jubilant if they could have seen who was lurking just a short distance behind them. It was Fire on his way to the village to take his wife and children with him. He needed someone to cook his food and to dress the skins he brought in. The cave he dug was only a hole in the cliff. His wife could make it deep and fine for him. Because of all this, Fire decided to brave the village to bring his family out. He chuckled to himself as he heard the singing and thought of how surprised Ulf would be when he found that Fire's family had disappeared in the night.

The women of Pang were sitting around the council fire, worrying. It had been many days, and they had no word of their men.

"Perhaps they were wiped out," said Buck Tooth. She always looked at the worst side of things.

Sand turned to her. "Buck Tooth, I'm surprised at you. It's a long way up there, and it takes time to get there and back."

"Ah well," sighed Buck Tooth, "Ulf was probably killed anyhow. The chief is always in the front of the fight."

That was too much for Sand. She went over to Buck Tooth and scratched at her face. Buck Tooth yelled and grabbed Sand's hair. A fine fight was beginning when Jet ran into the circle.

"They are coming! I hear them singing!" The two women forgot their grudge, laughed, and ran forward to meet the victorious men of Pang.

It was a joyous homecoming for most of the tribe, except for the women who had to ask, "Where is One Eye?" or "Where is my husband?" They could not join in the merriment. They were widows now, and when their children were grown, they would have to live in their caves, and that was never as pleasant as having one's own.

The men rested for the remainder of the day. That night, they would have a big feast of the reindeer and tell the story of the great battle and the herdsmen of the north.

Dog found Jet in the same place he left her–by the oak on the river's edge. "Jet, here is the arrow. I didn't have to use it. I saved it until last so I could bring it home to you if we won."

Jet took the arrow. "I'm glad. I was afraid all the time you would be killed."

"Will you sit next to me tonight at the feast?"

"I thought you didn't want girls around."

"Oh, that was then. I guess I changed my mind. You are all right."

"Then I will." Jet smiled and ran home. She was delighted Dog wouldn't snub her anymore. He was more fun to play with than the girls. He taught her birdcalls, how to make friends with the small animals, and how to shoot a bow and arrow. When girls got together to play, it was fun to play with the dolls and tools, but still, they often created many rules, fought and went home in a huff.

Dog set his antlers on the shelf beside the saber-toothed tiger's head. They made a very imposing couple. Later he would fix it so it would last as he had with the tiger. Dog's method of preserving these heads was very simple. He scooped out the inside and put bright pebbles in the eye sockets. Then he filled the heads with clay from the river's edge and let it dry. Afterwards, they were ready to sit on the shelf and glare at everyone who entered.

Fire watched the feast. He was hungry, but he could not go in and demand the best as he had before. The fire was warm, and he was cold. He missed his place close to the flames on the opposite side of the smoke. He heard Ulf sing of his victory, and he laughed. Was he, Fire, not still alive? He heard Fern tell of how he killed the reindeer, and the aroma from that same animal made Fire's greedy mouth water. It seemed they would never give up their laughing, eating, or dancing.

Several hours later, the last family went to its cave, and Fire stole into the village. First, he stopped at the stripped carcass and hunted for a piece of meat that might be left. There was none. He shrugged his shoulders and went on up to what had been his own cave. His wife was awake, and when she saw who was entering the cave, she calmed down and helped him wake the children. He piled all of his belongings on their backs. He carried nothing. His family didn't mind. He had always been like that, and when he told them to follow him, they picked up their packs and followed him out into the frosty night.

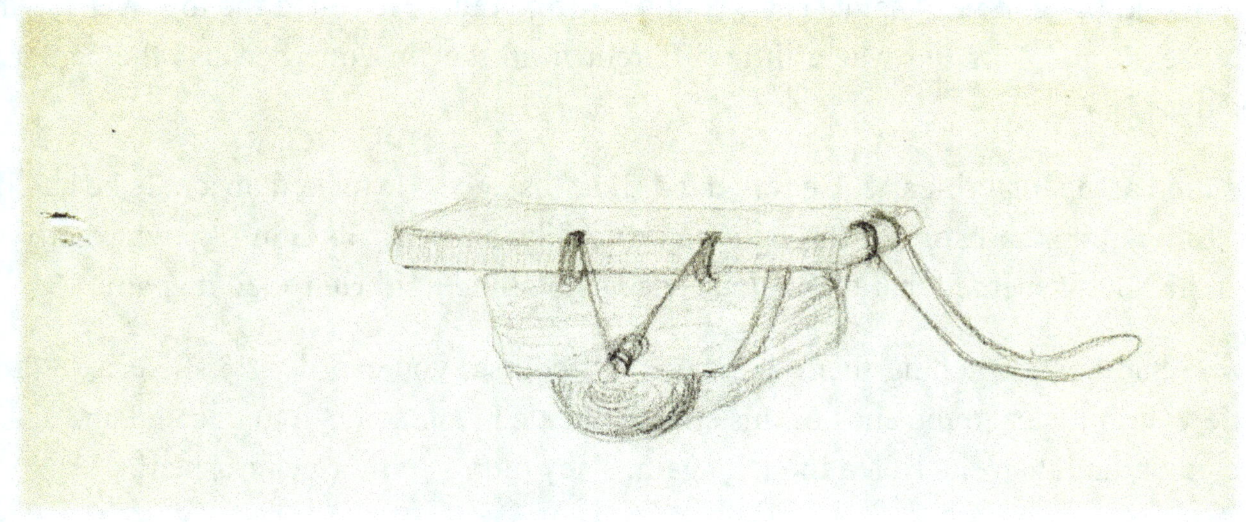

Chapter Six:

The Carrying Log

Dog, Tabat, and Jet were playing halfheartedly down by the river. There just didn't seem to be anything to amuse them. Tabat was staring absentmindedly at a short log, when he suddenly remembered how he and Dog had experimented earlier, trying to make such a log carry bundles. He jumped up.

"I've got it!" he yelled.

"For the sake of the great sun mammoth, what?" asked Jet, but Dog had followed Tabat's gaze, which didn't give him time to answer Jet.

"Yes!" he shouted. "We have lots of time now. We can really figure out a way to do it!"

"Do what?" questioned Jet. "Do hurry and tell me!"

"Oh, that's right," said Dog. "You weren't with us. We were trying to make a log carry bundles."

"How foolish," said Jet. "You can't do that."

"We don't know that yet," said Tabat, "but we'll find out." He rolled the log over to where they were sitting. This log was a little different from the first one because the center had rotted away.

Dog stared at the log critically. He rolled it a short distance. He picked up a pole he had been using for vaulting and stuck it through the center like an axle. He didn't know exactly why he did this, but it seemed that that hole needed something in it. He rolled it again.

Jet, who had been watching them, laughed. "Of course, you can do it!" she cried. "Look. Just tie your bundles to the ends of this stick." She tied Dog's pouch to one end and Tabat's to the other, and then she rolled the log again. They didn't spill or get crushed!

Dog waved his arms in the air and danced. "We've got it! We've got it!" he sang out.

"You mean I got it," said Jet.

But Tabat saw a difficulty. "How are you going to get this log to go where you want it to?" he asked.

Dog frowned.

Jet frowned.

Tabat frowned.

"We have to think," said Dog.

Jet smiled. "Have either of you a long, stout, leather thong?" she asked.

"Yes, I have," said Tabat.

"Well, get it!" she exclaimed.

Tabat ran off in the direction of his home. It wasn't very long before he came back, panting heavily. If it weren't for his curiosity, he probably would have walked. Jet had a reason for not telling him why she wanted the thong.

Triumphantly, she tied one end of the thong to one end of the stick. She carried the other end of the thong to the other end of the shaft and tied it there. She stood with her hands on her hips, surveying her handiwork.

"Well?" asked Dog.

"Pull it, you empty heads!"

Slowly Dog caught the idea, and he grinned as its simplicity came home to him. He picked up the thong and pulled it behind him. The log bumped over the grass and carried the two pouches tied to its axle. The children had invented the first wheel!

They trundled their little wagon into the village, and soon the whole tribe of Pang was exclaiming at the wonder of it. It wouldn't be very long before every family owned a carrying log.

Old Bearclaw, who was now medicine man, examined the discovery and pronounced it good magic. That was the last obstacle in the path of the young inventors. If he had said it was bad magic, they would have had to burn it lest evil demons did something terrible to the tribe! Now they proudly carried every bundle tied to the carrying pole, no matter how small.

Ulf was not satisfied with the invention. This log was small, and the pole close to the ground. That wouldn't be suitable for carrying something as large as an animal's carcass. He had a feeling the children had made something very important, but it wasn't finished. He knew that if he took a big log, it would be as hard to pull it as to carry the animal. He talked to Sand about it, but she thought the little wheel was marvelous just as it was and could offer no new suggestions. Ulf was baffled. He thought about it in all of his spare time, but he could not improve the device. However, he would not give up. While everyone was taking the log for granted, Ulf still pondered. Someday, he felt sure, he would discover something that would finish this invention.

Dog awoke one day and felt there was something different from the day before. He was not cold; the warm indoor fire took care of that need. He was not hungry, for even if this was a season of scarcity, they had meat traded from the Reindeer tribe. But there was something definitely strange happening. He went to the entrance of the cave and looked out. Then he knew; he had smelled the clear, tingly air that arrived with snow!

It seemed Dog had toes on his hands; he was so clumsy putting on his feet-skins. He finally got them on and was running outside when Sand's voice called him back. She was holding a fine wolf skin.

"Dog, I am going to tie this across your shoulders; you need it out there in the snow."

"Aw, I'm not cold. I can't run or throw snowballs with all this on! I'm not a girl!"

"You do as I say!" She wrapped the skin around his shoulders and pushed him outside. There he stood, scowling. Trying to make a girl out of him–that's what she was doing. How could he face Tabat or Fox Ear with this–this thing on his shoulders? He picked up a handful of snow and idly fashioned a round ball. It was fine snow and would pack well. But he wouldn't have any fun. The boys would laugh at him and call him his mother's baby.

The glade was completely covered and untracked. The branches of the trees were heavy with snow, and the air was full of big, fat flakes. He heard sharp, happy barks and saw Puppy and Knife Tooth rolling in the snow and biting at it. Then Dog had to laugh. Sand had tied a small foot-skin on each paw of the two pets! She even tried to make babies out of the wolves!

"What are you laughing at?" challenged a cross voice, and Dog saw Tabat sitting with his back to him. Across his shoulders was the curly hide of a wild goat! Dog ran over to him.

"I'm not laughing at you. See? I have one, too. I was laughing at the two dogs. They have feet-skins on. I guess mothers just like to make you so heavy with pelts that you can't even run!"

Then Tabat had to laugh. Both felt better now that there were two of them. They laughed still more when Fox Ear, Bowleg, Leaf, Bat, and all the rest came slowly out of their caves looking like thunderclouds, all wearing a fur pelt across their shoulders! Of course, the girls wore pelts, too, but they liked them. Some even had skins tied to their hands, and then they weren't much good at throwing snowballs.

The boys discussed this common failing of mothers for a while and then forgot all about it as they chose sides for a fine snowball war. Dog was one chief and Fox Ear the other. They built a wall in the center of their glade, and Fox Ear's tribe was to stay behind it and keep it from being captured.

Even the girls joined in, for when snow was on the ground, everyone was equal. Later on in the day, even the men and women would be out pummeling each other with the white snow. There was no hunting or skins to be tanned, and this was a fine way to keep warm!

Dog would have to use strategy. He gathered his men around him as he had seen Ulf do. He divided his party into two groups. One was to attack from the front, while the other came up from the rear and surprised their enemy team. Tabat was to lead the rear forces while Dog brought up the frontal attack. As they talked, the boys made snowballs to carry.

Behind the wall, Fox Ear and his army were also busy piling up ammunition. They didn't know what to expect, as they were on the defensive.

Dog yelled. He and his men rushed into the open, pounding snowballs on the fort. The ones inside promptly gave them a dose of their own medicine right back. Bat tried to storm the walls, but Leaf pushed him, sending him sprawling. Leaf got a fine face full of snow as a reward. The glade wasn't untrammeled now!

Puppy and Knife Tooth joined the fun. They barked and ran from one boy to the other. They were a long way from the wolves that cold and hunger drove to madness! Instead of being a bitter enemy, the snow was a good playfellow to these animals. Why, it didn't even form lumps in their pads because of the feet-skins the kind humans had provided!

Dog yelled. He and his men
rushed into the open, pounding
snowballs at the fort.

Dog gave a howl that was the signal for Tabat's advance. He and the rest of the children crept silently across the glade. They didn't want to be noticed until they were inside the fort, and it seemed they would succeed. Fox Ear's tribe was very busy repulsing the advances of Dog and his army. It was Puppy who would be thanked for the end of that war. He saw the forms of the boys and girls crawling through the snow. He ran back, barking all the way. Even Dog's agonized shout could not make him return. Puppy was worried about Tabat, who was not walking as he should. He pranced up to his friend and grabbed him by the shoulder skin. He seemed to be saying, "Get up, Tabat, get up!"

Tabat gave Puppy a push. "Go back," he whispered, but the damage was done. Fox Ear's side had seen the others.

"Charge!" shouted Tabat. It was the only thing to do. Scooping up snow and making snowballs as they ran, Tabat's party charged! At the same time, Dog's group stormed the wall! They laughed, shouted, wrestled, and washed each other's faces in the snow. The battle had turned rough and tumble! Nobody won, and nobody lost. It was great fun! When they were tired, they all sat behind the fort and rested for a few minutes before they went home and loudly demanded food.

Sand was just dumping the heated stones into the large hollow one when Dog entered the cave, red-cheeked and hungry. Ulf was sitting on a pile of furs and watching her while he gave little Sky a ride on his foot. Sand used a small piece of fur to protect her hands from the hot stones. But the fur slipped, and she touched the rock with her bare hand.

"Ulf, you do that," she said crossly, putting her burnt fingers into her mouth. Ulf thought she looked very pretty when she was angry, or else he would never have acted so unlike a chief by helping his wife with her work. He smiled and picked up the little fur.

"Why don't you just heat the big hollow stone?" he asked. The method Sand used seemed irksome.

"I tried it, but the stone is too big. It puts the fire out when I set something in the flames."

"Oh," was all Ulf said, but he had something else to ponder. He tossed the rock holder to Sand. "Here," he said. "Do it yourself." Ulf went back to his bed and gravely studied the ceiling.

In the afternoon, everyone went outdoors with their sliding bones. These were rib bones of different large animals. They had been scraped nearly flat on the outside of the curve, and holes had been bored through them. Most of the men had mammoth bones. They tied them to their feet with thongs, and while squatting low, they could slide down a hill or a small grade. It was a great sport. Some of the men with the mammoth sliding bones could stand up and jump on them. That day Ulf brought a new thing with him. He had taken two of the bones and tied them to a flat piece of wood. When they arrived at the top of a small, unobstructed hill, Ulf sat Sky on this device and gave it a push. Sky hung on and shouted breathlessly. The new toy was a success!

All that day, the people made the most of the year's first snowfall. Later the grown-ups got tired of the play, but the children loved it. It seemed the winters were shorter every year, and they had to enjoy them while they lasted. This year the people were especially happy. They didn't have to face a food shortage because of the agreement with the herdsmen.

Bearclaw watched Ulf's little sled, and he considered it carefully. Ulf had spoken to him many times about the unfinished carrying log, and while watching this new invention, Bearclaw seemed to sense the answer to the question. If he could only tie the two ideas together!

Bearclaw called Ulf over, and they retired to his cave. He told him his ideas and said, "If we could only tie them together!"

"That's it!" said Ulf. "Tie them together."

"The ideas? What do you mean, Ulf?"

"No—the slide board and the carrying log. Look." Ulf ran outside and brought in the slide board. "I will take this home tonight, and tomorrow I shall make a carrying board!"

Bearclaw nodded. "How are you going to do it?"

"I don't know where to tie it yet, but I'll think it out."

"But I know," said Bearclaw. "Let me keep this tonight."

Ulf agreed. It was right that the medicine man should figure the way to tie the two together. Ulf left the sled at the cave of wise, old Bearclaw. He felt a weight off his mind because, at last, the carrying log would finally be finished.

All night Bearclaw sat by his fire with the two inventions, many leather thongs, stone chisels, knives, bores, and other tools. The ends of the log were ragged because they had been broken from a tree. Bearclaw took his chisel and made the two ends smooth. Again, he shoved the axle through the log and measured it with his hands. The log was too long. He chopped two hands' length from it and pushed the axle through. It was just right.

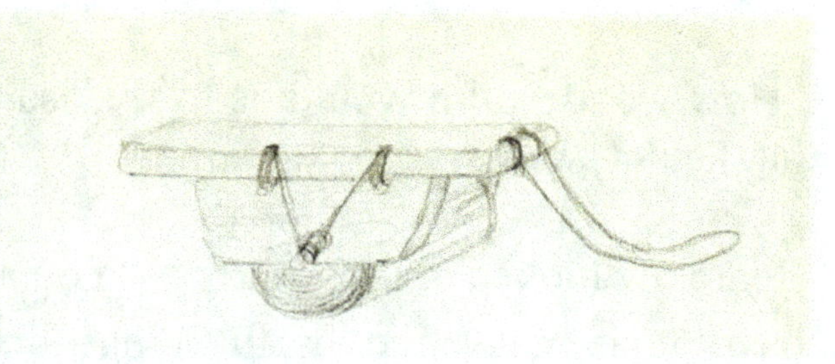

Ulf had bored holes in the piece of wood he used as a platform to tie the runners to. "That was good work," thought Bearclaw. The main job now was to bore a large hole through each runner. It seemed too bad to spoil a pair of fine bones like that when wood was better suited for the purpose. He loosened the bones and laid them aside. It didn't take him long to carve two rectangles of wood and bore small holes near the top of each. He bored a big hole in the center of each as well before he tied them where the bones had been. He put the ends of the axle through the big holes and prepared to tie all this onto the platform. Then Bearclaw was disgusted. The log was too big to fit! He would have to make larger sidepieces.

Bearclaw knew what he was doing, and before long, he had it all put together. A wagon! He then found that tying the pull-thong to the axle caused the platform to tip, and when he bored holes in the platform and tied the thong there, the axle slipped from its mooring. This was a new difficulty and puzzled the old man. He had promised a carrying board by morning. Ulf's faith in him as a medicine man might be shaken if he did not have one ready. Suddenly the idea came to him. It meant boring another hole in the middle of each side of the platform, and that was long work with his crude tools. The sun had appeared over the hill when they tied a thong around each end of the axle and through the holes in the platform. The carrying board was finished!

Later Bearclaw proudly exhibited his work to the tribe, and murmurs of praise for this medicine man were heard all through the crowd. Although Bearclaw and the tribe did not realize it, this little invention had made a great stride in man's progress. The wagon took the burden from a man's back. They thought only of how wonderful it would be able to pull their bundles instead of carrying them. As time passed, they devised a wagon with two logs, which kept it from tipping. After that, they created one with four logs cut narrowly, like a wheel, but these greater contraptions came much later... Bearclaw gave the first one to Dog, which he and Tabat used to pull Jet around by hitching themselves to it. They called her the best bundle.

Ulf, Dog, and Bearclaw were standing on the river's edge one day, watching a few late birds in their flight to the warmer lands.

"How wonderful it would be to fly," said Ulf. "I wish I could make wings for myself."

Bearclaw looked at him sharply. "You are a wise man, my son, and have made many fine, useful things–but flying! That is impossible and bad magic to even think about."

Ulf nodded. Bearclaw was right; flying was bad magic, and yet, how wonderful it would be! Dog looked at old Bearclaw. He knew that in his heart, the medicine man, too, envied the birds. It would be nice to swoop low into the wind and rise again before an enemy death stick could get you.

Bearclaw turned. "Bad magic, my son, forget it." And he went toward the village. Ulf and Dog watched the birds flying swiftly over the snowfields.

"See Dog, they can follow the sun mammoth while we have to stay here in the snow."

"But we like the snow. Birds can't shout, or dance, or speak. We eat them, so I guess they aren't so lucky."

"They can fly, Dog. And if we could do that, then we would be the masters of everything. Oh, well, forget it. It's bad magic anyhow. People will never fly."

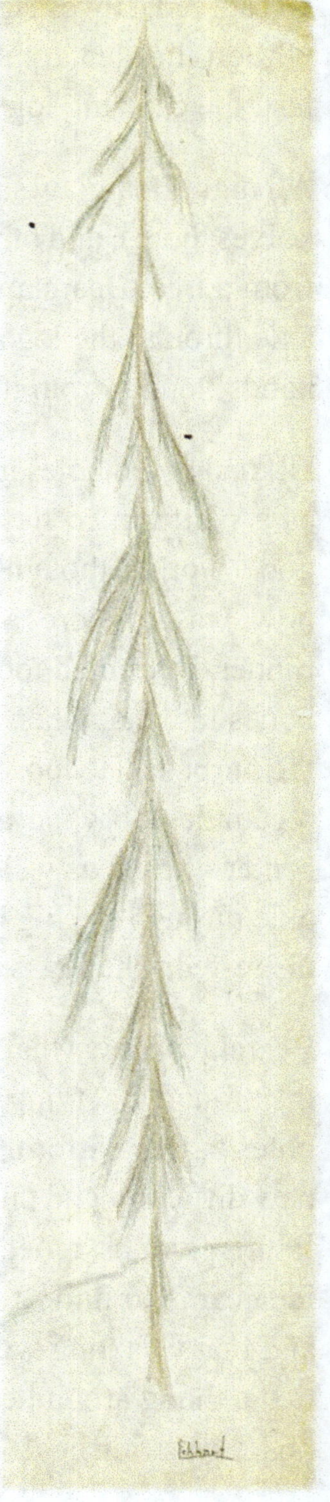

The two were silent, and Dog felt immensely grown up to be talked to like that. Thinking of flying was bad magic, yet they did not go home until the last bird had flown overhead and cast a long shadow on the snow.

Chapter Seven:

Springtime

It was morning. Ulf and Dog were again watching the birds, but this time they were coming back to the more northern countries. There was snow now only in patches in the valleys. The wind was sharp, but when it died a little, the sun sent its warmth to the people. It was the waking up season, the second since Dog had found Puppy. Knife Tooth was fully grown and followed Puppy everywhere. It was strange the two wolves weren't with Dog and his father that morning.

"Come on, let's go back to the village," suggested Dog, for Ulf was muttering to himself.

"If I tied a pair of skins to my arms…," Ulf continued under his breath. Dog was worried. He didn't want his father to play with bad magic. Ulf laughed. "All right, Dog. You needn't worry. I won't do anything."

They were interrupted by Jet, who was so excited she couldn't speak. She jumped up and down, laughed, and pointed toward the village. The two followed her and were surprised when they came to the cave. Every child in Pang was gathered around, talking. They pushed through the crowd and found Puppy and Knife Tooth on guard. They were guarding eight small wolf cubs!

"See?" exclaimed Jet. "Baby Puppies!"

"Knife Tooth won't let us touch them," said Tabat. "Only Sand. She lets her pick them up." Knife Tooth and Puppy growled when anyone except Sand or Dog approached. Dog looked at the tiny cubs.

"Their eyes! They have no eyes!" he exclaimed. Ulf looked closely. Dog was right. The puppies had no eyes! Dog was disappointed. He had been so proud of the cubs, only now to discover they had no eyes. It was too bad!

"We can keep them, anyhow, can't we?" he asked.

Little Sky echoed, "Can't we?" He repeated everything he heard Dog say these days. Sky was two years old now and adored his big brother, who was now eleven.

"See what your mother says." Ulf didn't want to tell the children they would kill the little cubs, so he put the responsibility on Sand.

"Well, I think we might keep them for a while. They are the first wolves born tame, and I think we should take care of them. Maybe they will grow eyes later."

Dog put his arms around his mother. He hated the thought of killing the squirmy little things. They had such funny noses, they tumbled over each other, and their milky teeth were so white and sharp. It was no wonder Dog felt proud of them, even though they didn't have eyes.

The rest of the children were disappointed too. They trickled away, saying they didn't want any blind cubs. Soon only Dog, Jet, Tabat, and Fox Ear were left. They decided they would raise the cubs, eyes or no eyes, and each could have two. Sand heard the plot and objected. She already had two wolves in her cave, and two more were just too many. Other homes would have to be found, and that was final! Dog sighed and looked at the cubs. Oh well, he would have them all for a little while.

Dog counted the cubs as soon as he awoke each morning. They were always there. Sand had fixed a large bearskin for Knife Tooth to lie on, and she was very particular that the cubs didn't roam. On the eighth morning, Dog couldn't believe his sight. Every cub looked at him through bright blue eyes!

"Jet!" he called. "Tabat! Fox Ear! Quick! They have eyes!" All the children heard him and ran up to the cave. The cubs were fine now, and they all wanted to own puppies. But Dog was firm. They laughed at the little wolf family once, and he didn't forget that. He named the three lucky ones who should receive cubs, and added the other two were going to Bearclaw because he was a good medicine man and fond of Puppy.

The children brought fine pieces of meat to Knife Tooth and cooked roots and herbs, stolen from their own cooking stones. The cubs waxed fat, and soon Knife Tooth could no longer keep them to the confines of the bearskin. They played and tumbled all over the cave, but Dog thought they weren't yet big enough to give away. He wanted to keep them for as long as possible.

Dog was glad the air was growing warmer. The hateful shoulder skins were put back into the beds, and soon they wouldn't even have to wear feet skins. Dog had tried to sneak out without them yesterday, but Sand had caught him and made him put them on.

The next day he did get away, and Dog took Sky for a ride on his back. They galloped up and down the riverbank, and Sky laughed and hit Dog's back with his tiny fists. The mud felt good against Dog's feet, and he sang. Sky imitated him. Puppy and Knife Tooth left their family for a while and joined them. The waking-up season was in their blood, and they all tingled with the urge to run, jump, and make noise. There were some girls down the river away making tiny bowls for their carved wooden dolls. Jet was with them. She had a particularly fine doll. Her father carved it in pieces and tied them together so the joints moved. Dog was disgusted. He didn't see why girls played such silly games. Singing to empty wooden-headed dolls when they could be singing about hunting or running was very odd. Sky agreed with him perfectly. Sky always agreed. Dog shouted cheerily at the girls, and he and Sky hunted for Ulf. They saw him talking to Bearclaw in front of the old man's cave. The two boys were nearly there when they saw an old woman come up to Ulf.

"Oh, Chief," she exclaimed, "the good spirit has visited the cave of Ulf, and it brought a girl baby with it!" Ulf jumped up and ran toward his cave. Dog and Sky watched him. Dog smiled. A little sister! He had always wanted a little sister. With Sky still on his back, he raced through the village. He wanted to see the new arrival. He hoped she was pretty, like Jet.

Dog was beaming as he entered the cave, but when he saw the little sister, his face straightened out. He just looked at her. She was small and red, and she didn't have any hair! She looked just like Sky had looked when he was born, only worse because she was thinner and more wrinkled. Why, even Jet's new sister hadn't been as bad as this!

Sand and Ulf thought the baby was beautiful, and Dog was saddened. His parents–the chief of the tribe–how could they be satisfied? Why didn't they send it back? Surely the spirits had another they could bring. Then Dog thought of the wolf cubs. Maybe she would grow hair, and she would smooth out a little bit. Sky didn't look bad now. Maybe she would change. Fox Ear's little brother had had hair, curly hair, just like Fox Ear's. Dog walked out of the cave, kicked a stone, and it landed several feet away. Sky followed him, and he kicked a stone. It didn't move. Sky sat on the ground and cried about his stubbed toe. For once, Dog didn't care. He just picked Sky up, and then Dog left his brother standing there as he strode down to the glade. Sky was surprised and couldn't decide whether to cry or not. He decided he wouldn't, and instead, he followed his brother.

Dog whistled for Puppy, and they started out toward the woods. The leaves were beginning to turn green, and a few more rains would bring them all out. It would also bring flowers. Dog loved bright colours, and the flowers were the source of most of it in the area. The more brilliant they were, the better he liked them. He knew of a deep glen where many gorgeous plants grew. He and Puppy headed there. He didn't notice Sky a little way behind him. They had walked only a short distance when Tabat dropped out of a tree in front of them. He had been gathering bird's eggs and eating them. He decided to go along with Dog and listened to his sad tale of the ugly little sister. He did not see Sky trotting along in the rear either.

Tabat agreed that Dog certainly did have bad luck, and he wondered why Ulf and Sand should be so pleased. Still, perhaps his new sister would improve. They both clung to the theory that Sky had certainly looked awful when he was new. Their hopes raised a little, and they walked a little faster. The air was pleasant, and there was snow only in the shady glens now.

They skirted a disguised pit that was used as an animal trap. If they had not helped dig it, then they might have been caught themselves. It was certainly a beautiful trap.

Only a minute later, they heard a crash and a cry. "An animal! It's been following us!" exclaimed Tabat, as he, Dog, and Puppy ran toward the trap.

"How will we get it out? We have no thongs."

"Let's look at it anyhow." Dog reached the edge and peered in. "It's Sky! He must have followed us! How will we get him out?" Sky was crying. The leaves and branches had broken his fall somewhat, but he was still hurt.

"Dog!" he cried. "Dog! Dog!"

"I'm here," answered Dog. "Wait." He and Tabat sat on the brink of the pit and thought. How would they get him out with no thongs?

Tabat jumped up. "I know! See that little tree there on the other edge?

You hang onto that, and I will lower myself into the pit from your legs, and then you can stand on my shoulders and get down."

"All right, brainy one, how do we get out again?"

"I never thought of that." Tabat was troubled. He sat down again. Sky yelled and screamed for his brother.

"Dog," said Tabat, "why couldn't we come up the same way we went down? You could put Sky on your shoulders, and then you climb up on my shoulders and out. You can set him on the ground and hang your feet down for me to climb out!" "Yes! It will work. Tabat, you really have a brain!"

So down they went. Dog was glad he wasn't an animal. It was harder than they had thought; Tabat had to jump a little, and it was hard for Dog to reach his shoulders, but they made it without a mishap, and soon they were at the bottom of the pit. Dog remembered the way the diggers made their way out with thongs tied to the little tree. These thongs had sticks tied to them at intervals. The men used those to climb up on.

Sky was only bruised, and when he saw Dog, he felt much better. Dog put him on his back and told him to hang on tight. Dog then climbed up on Tabat's shoulders and reached for the edge. He reached again before he dared look up. He knew what he would find when he did. There was the rim, at least a foot above the tips of Dog's fingers!

Dog climbed down, and he and Tabat looked at each other.

"Well?" asked Dog.

"Well!" said Tabat.

Puppy, from up above, raced around the pit, barking and growling. He wanted the boys to come up.

"Puppy!" shouted Dog. "Go get Ulf! Get Ulf!"

Puppy barked and lay down at the edge of the trap.

"Oh, Puppy, why don't you bring Ulf?"

Puppy pricked his ears. 'Bring Ulf' made sense to him. 'Go get Ulf' was something he didn't understand. He rose and trotted in the direction of Pang. The boys sat down to wait. They felt very silly, caught in a trap they helped build!

"Why don't we go?" asked Sky when he saw them sit.

"Because Tabat hasn't the brain he thought he has."

"What's a brain?" asked Sky.

"Tabat wouldn't know."

"It wasn't my fault; you said it would work."

"I know it. We have to wait for Ulf, Sky."

"Ulf? That's my father." Sky laughed. If Ulf were coming, it would be all right. Besides, wasn't Dog with him? Sky was no longer afraid, and he fell asleep.

Puppy ran all the way back to Pang and entered Ulf's cave. There he didn't even stop to glance at Knife Tooth and the cubs, but went straight to Ulf, grabbed his fur, and pulled. Ulf waved him away. Puppy went to the entrance of the cave, barked, and then he came back and pulled at Ulf again.

"What ails that dog?" asked Ulf crossly. Jet's mother was there, and she remembered Dog and Puppy going into the woods together. Now Puppy was alone and she noted how odd it seemed. Ulf then jumped up and, without a word, started to follow the now happy Puppy.

Dog heard Puppy bark, and soon the prisoners saw the anxious face of Ulf peering over the edge. Dog explained the predicament and how they happened to be there, and Sky proudly echoed him.

At the finish of the recital, Ulf scratched his head. Then he said, "Dog, get back on Tabat's shoulders and hand Sky up to me. Tabat can hang on to your feet, and I will drag you both up."

Dog nearly fell off of Tabat when he handed Sky up to his father, who was leaning over the rim. Ulf had brought no thongs with him, so he had to use his own strength to get the boys out of the hole. He told Tabat to hold onto Dog's ankles, and he pulled Dog up by the wrists. Tabat's arms had to reach up before he left the ground, so Dog was nearly halfway out when the extra weight jerked Ulf's arm. Ulf stood up and pulled. The edge of the pit scraped Dog's stomach, and it seemed Tabat was going to tear his ankles apart!

Slowly Ulf pulled Dog out until he could see Tabat's hands just above the rim. He dared not let go of Dog, or they would both fall back into the trap. Dog felt like a rope! Tabat felt as though he just couldn't hold on any longer, but soon he was out to his waist. He was then able to let go and scrambled out the rest of the way himself. Dog lay flat on the ground where he was dropped and Ulf sat leaning against the little tree. Only Sky, who caused the mishap, wasn't tired. He had a few black and blue marks where he hit the branches as he fell, but that was all.

On the way back to the village, Ulf asked Dog why he didn't like his new sister. Dog explained, and Ulf looked at him. "You should have seen yourself! I wanted to take you out and feed you to the wolves. You weren't red—you were purple. And you wrinkled your face and yelled. I never thought that a future chief could have such a son. You see, I wasn't chief then, but later on, my father joined the spirit world, and after that, I became chief. You are a good son now, so I think the new one will be all right, too."

Dog felt better when he heard that, and he began to think maybe the baby wasn't so bad after all. Perhaps she would even grow up to be as pretty as Jet. Tabat thought so too, and by the time they reached the village, they firmly believed the little sister was the best baby ever to join the tribe of Pang.

All the children gathered around the day Dog gave Jet her two cubs. She named them Bark and Bite because that is exactly what they did. Dog felt the puppies should be given away slowly, so he waited a week before he told Tabat he might pick out his two. He decided to call them Grey Runner and Thunderbolt because wolves were fierce, and even though his were tame, he wanted them to have big wild names. Strangely enough, these two were the gentlest and tamest of all, and Tabat, even though he felt silly about it, pampered them even more than Puppy was pampered.

Fox Ear's mother was a little dubious about the idea of having two big animals in her cave, but when Fox Ear brought home the two furry cubs, she relented and said he could keep them. Later, she grew very fond of them. They were called Sunshine and Shadow, because one had bright fur while the other's coat was dull and smoky.

Dog took the last two cubs over to the cave of Bearclaw. The old man was very pleased that Dog should think of him. He had many ideas of what he could do with the intelligent mind of the tame wolves. He named them Loyal and True, because he knew how good Puppy was, and he wanted his dogs to be just the same. Knife Tooth and Puppy didn't mind the cubs being spread around because they were all in the same village, and they all played together in a most complicated game of chasing each other and seeing who could bark the most.

The air was beginning to smell of green trees and new grass instead of snowfields and cold winds from the north. The animals were coming out of hiding, and the reindeer meat-weary people had more variety in their diet. One day a party of hunters brought home two giant sloths, and another day a big bear was brought to the tribe. Yet, in spite of this good luck, Ulf felt the urge to go out again. He knew that to the north and toward the sunrise, there was a great area of forest that he had not entered. He decided to take some men and go exploring. Sand, of course, was against it. She was never completely happy unless her family was home and safe, but Ulf wanted to be off, and Bearclaw had said the adventure was good magic. They packed great bundles of meat and weapons onto some carrying logs, and Bearclaw had a ceremonial dance for them.

All during these preparations they did not notice the two rogues, Dog and Tabat. The boys crept off in corners by themselves and talked a great deal. Pretty soon Jet was gathering with them, and the three went up to an old cave nobody lived in because it was so dark. Here they would take little bundles, stay for a long time, and come out without them. Whenever talk of the expedition was going on, they would look at each other and giggle.

The men decided to take Puppy and Knife Tooth along because the presence of two wolves doing their bidding would help frighten any people they encountered who might be hostile. Ulf went about singing, and he told Sand not to worry. Hadn't he always come back before? Why should he want to die and leave his nice family? Sand would have to smile and promise to think it was all right. The village would not be empty of men, and Bearclaw would be there. She decided not to fret, and yet she was so worried that she didn't notice Dog's strange activities. Even when they went fishing with their spears with the barbed bone ends instead of flint points, Dog, Tabat, and Jet were together and talking in a low tone. They would stand in the river and plunge their harpoons into the water when a fish swam by. More often than not, they would catch the fish. That spring, Sand taught all the women in the village how to fish and like the new food. By doing that, she could keep her mind off of the trip, which was coming closer every day.

Finally, one night they had a great dance for good luck, and the carrying boards were brought out to get all ready to go. In the morning, the men started out, singing loudly, and they didn't notice they were pulling one extra carrying board.

Chapter Eight:

The Expedition

It was Fern, the father of Tabat, who first noticed the strange actions of the wolves. They stuck close by the heaviest carrying board and occasionally reared up on their hind claws and smelled it. They whined when they did this. This went on for a day and a half before Fern spoke of it to Ulf.

"Fern, how many carrying boards did we have?" asked Ulf.

"As many as the fingers on one hand with no thumb."

Ulf looked at the carts and figured. "How odd–there are enough now for a hand with a thumb. There is an extra cart here! Open the one that the dogs are making all the fuss over."

The men untied the thongs slowly. *Perhaps there could be evil spirits in the cart. Perhaps a wild animal would jump out. Perhaps anything!* Ulf grew impatient. As soon as the thongs were loosened, he jerked the fur covering off, revealing Dog and Tabat!

Ulf just looked at them, then took his son by the ear and led him over to a fallen log. Fern followed with Tabat. The men sat down together on the log, and both turned their sons over their knees, bottom side up!

The spanking was administered with a will. When it was over, the boys felt very embarrassed. Their dignities, as well as their anatomies, were hurt.

"Now," said Ulf, "you start right home. Your mothers will be worried sick. How did you get tied up in there, anyhow?"

"Jet tied us in. And our mothers won't worry, honest. Jet told them where we were. Oh, please let us come!"

Ulf looked at Fern. It was clever of the boys. But no–they had been told to stay home. Then, one of the men said they should be allowed to come along. And another man thought so too.

"Well, all right. But you must do as I say and not be a nuisance," Ulf relented, smiling. He was really very proud of the boys. After that, the boys had to pull their own carrying log up to the reindeer village. There they would leave it until the return trip—no use taking an empty cart.

Dar welcomed them royally and prepared a feast. He was amazed at the carrying boards. As Dar and the Pang men talked, Ulf noticed a reindeer being driven down the center of the village. It was pulling a bundle of sticks. Every once in a while, the thong would break from being dragged on the ground, and the woman who drove the beast would stop and tie it up again. Then she spied Ulf's empty carrying board and pulled it over to the reindeer. She tied her sticks to the board, hitched the cart to the reindeer, and unconcernedly drove off.

Ulf was astounded. "Dar, I will give your tribe our extra carrying log and these knives I brought for as many tame reindeer as I can count on one hand without the thumb."

Dar thought the proposal over. With one carrying board, they could make many like it. And they needed knives. "Yes," he nodded, "with as many bows and death sticks as I have feet." These people had learned to shoot, but were still unable to make bows and arrows. Ulf gave him the price, and they went up to the herd. Dar picked out four fine bucks, and they brought them down to the village. Then, Dar showed them how to make the harness out of extra-wide thongs, and very soon, they were off again. Dar and Aki, another reindeer man, joined the party, and they set out toward the northeast, which they called the cold sunrise.

As they entered the uncharted forest, Ulf chopped gashes into trees at intervals. He did that so that if they got lost, then they could find their way home again. The woods were thick, and the men had to go ahead of the animals to cut away through the underbrush. Vines tangled through the trees, and it seemed there was nothing but forest. Hunting was very good, and they didn't have to dig into their supplies at all except for water. It rained one night before their water gave out, and they hung the empty skins opened from the branches of trees. By morning, they were full again. Dog and Tabat were disgusted. There was no excitement at all! This was just monotonous; cutting through the forest and hardly moving.

A faint continuous roar filled their ears, but they didn't notice it at first. Then one day, Ulf declared that demons were howling in his head, and his ears were ringing. All the men found they heard the same noise, so they knew it was not in their heads. As they traveled the noise grew louder, and some of the men were afraid.

"The demons want us to go back! They are yelling at us! This is bad magic!"

But Bearclaw had said this was good magic, and Bearclaw knew. Ulf insisted they go forward, and although they were afraid, it was still better than going back alone. So, the men followed Ulf as the roar grew louder and louder. They noticed the forest was not as thick, and there was an increasing growth of long, tough grass. The soil felt sandy under the feet of the men, and there was a tangy smell in the air. There were no trees at all now! Dog and Tabat ran up over a small dune, and what they saw took their breath away! It was the sea! The roar had been the pounding of the surf, and the smell was that of clams, salt, seaweed, and spray!

"Oh, it's cold! Colder than the
river, but it's exciting!

The men came up behind the boys and stood, awestruck at the size of it! Water, as far as they could see! Knife Tooth and Puppy sniffed the exhilarating air and rolled in the sand. Dog and Tabat ran along the beach and into the surf.

"Oh-h-h, it's cold! Colder than the river, but it's exciting!" they called to the men who had come down to drink. The dogs and the reindeer would not touch the water, but the men took a long swallow. They were thirsty! But this water did not quench their thirst! It had an odd taste that they liked, even though it only made them thirstier. The taste seemed to satisfy a need in their bodies. They had never tasted salt before. Ulf decided this water was good medicine because it made them feel strong. They filed several skins with it and tied them to their carts.

Ulf noticed the dunes to the southeast rose into foothills, and then they soon became mountains. He wondered what could be over there. To the north was only water, so they decided to head into the hills. They didn't want to leave the pleasant sea, but Ulf wished to explore more unknowns. He would not go back to the village until he knew what was in those mountains!

They built a cairn on one of the dunes to show humans had been there. Then they built a fire on the beach, for they were going to stay there all night. It had been dark for several hours when a man jumped up, howling that he was wet. Soon they all found themselves lying in the water, and before long, their fire hissed and went out! The great sea had crept up on them and quenched it! The rest of the night, they sat on the dune, wide awake and full of fear, watching the tide come in across the beach. The sea was after them–it was angry! Ulf figured it was because they had taken some water, but then he noticed toward dawn that it was going backward--away from the men! But if it was not angry, why did it come up like that in the night?

Dog and Tabat watched the water rise and fall. They were as afraid as the rest that maybe it was after them. Maybe it didn't want them to run in the shallow surf! They, too, were surprised when it slithered back away from them.

"Perhaps," said Fern in the morning, "the big water eats the sand, and every night it comes up for its meal." The rest agreed. The sea had not been after them at all. It was a more comfortable thought than their first belief. They were sure Fern was right when they saw all their footprints had been erased during the night. Yes, the sea had been eating, not chasing them!

Again, they hitched the reindeer to the carrying boards and were off in the direction of the mountains. They'd had good luck so far, and they were happy. Dog, Tabat, Puppy, and Knife Tooth ran on ahead. The trip was looking up. Perhaps more exciting things would happen.

For two days, they traveled across the foothills, and they noticed that the hills grew steeper and higher. Now they were in a country of cliffs, deep valleys, and tall trees. Little rivulets dashed downhill until they tumbled over the edge of a precipice. The men clung to the sides of the mountain. They had to get below the carrying boards and hold them so they wouldn't tip over. The reindeer couldn't do it alone.

Again, Ulf was faced with a mutiny. The going was hard, and the men wanted to turn back, but Ulf was possessed with the idea to go forward and refused even to look back. Sometimes the slopes were not so steep, and they made better time. They saw a bear and a deer, and once, they spotted a clouded mountain leopard. However, they killed only enough to eat, as the carts were heavy enough as it was. A leopard was in a tree, and as the small procession passed under the limb, the cat sprang on the back of one of the reindeer, killing it instantly. Several men acted at once, and the great beast howled and fell to earth, studded with arrows. It was evening, so they camped right there. Ulf skinned the leopard and gave Puppy and Knife Tooth the carcass to eat. The people roasted the reindeer and ate most of it. The next morning, they finished the animal. They took the two skins and divided the load from the extra carrying board among the other three. Still, the burdens weren't too great. The meat was gone, and all they carried were pelts, weapons, and precious bags of salt water. Dog and Tabat took all the thongs off the old cart. These things were hard to make and should be saved.

With only the three reindeer that were left, they started again. Dog and Tabat were wide-eyed and alert. This trip was fun! Puppy and Knife Tooth ranged to all sides of the group, but they always came back. One night they howled at the moon, and Ulf grew worried. Suppose they went wild and killed them? But the following day, when Ulf fed them some of the meat he had brought back from a short forage into the woods, they ate it politely and licked his ear in thanks. The meat was an old nanny goat. She had two small kids. Ulf kept the kids alive. Goat skins were warm, and goat meat was very delicious. Ulf figured that with these two, he could raise goats much like the Reindeer tribe raised their animals. They tied a leather thong around each kid's neck so they could lead them and pressed farther into the mountains. The explorers crossed a valley where the grass was fresh and green. They stopped there to rest so the goats and reindeer could have a good meal. A stream ran through the center of the valley, and they all drank deep. The poor reindeer were quite worn out, and they laid down and fell asleep. The men agreed it would be better to stay there for the rest of the day and all night to give them a chance to rest.

That night, they heard wolves howling in the distance, and Puppy and Knife Tooth pricked their ears to listen to the call of their kind. Puppy whined and pawed at the ground. He wanted to join the pack. Knife Tooth slunk farther away from the fire. The old wolf fear was coming back to her. Dog and Tabat noticed these unusual actions and knew what they meant. Hastily they built a ring of campfires around the party. The two wolves would never dare to jump through the flames, and by morning they wouldn't want to. They talked to their pets all night, calling them by name and crooning to them. The sound of the beloved human voices stilled the whining and kept them close to the two boys. In the morning, the howling stopped, and the wolves became dogs again. The loyalty the humans had awakened in the hearts of these animals was too strong now to be overcome without a fight. Perhaps if Dog and Tabat had not kept talking and soothing the wolves, then they may have given in to their deep instincts. But the boys had calmed their animals, and so morning found the two tired dogs asleep inside the ring of fire.

Everyone felt better the next day after they had eaten a young deer that had ventured too close to the group. The reindeer were hitched up again, and the group started up the mountain on the other side of the valley. Near the bottom, the evergreen trees were tall and full. As they climbed, the men noticed the trees grew shorter and scrubbier and had a wind-tossed look. They climbed higher and higher, and the men had to get behind the carts and push. Even Dog and Tabat lent their smaller weights to the effort. The moon had been at its thinnest when they started out of Pang. The night they reached the timberline on the mountain, they noticed the moon man had become thin again. The tribesmen had been on the trail many, many days. In the morning, they started forward again but were not climbing anymore. They were still finding the unknown. The men had captured some of Ulf's spirit, and nothing could induce them to turn back now.

Down in the foothills and valleys, they had passed many glacier snouts, and the roaring noises had terrified them. These were believed to be the homes of the cold demons, and the men did not venture up to the mighty walls of ice. Now they found one of the wide, frozen rivers directly in front of them. A cold breeze blew from it, and looking up the glacier, they saw the huge, ragged mountain looking as though it might topple over onto them. The men were afraid. It was too big to be good magic! Dog and Tabat held each other's hands, and the feeling of another human being was comforting. They found that being up so high made their lungs hurt and their hearts beat faster. Dar complained of dizziness in his head. Even Ulf stood on the brink of the glacier and considered their course of action. The men felt very small to be trying to fight the enormous glacier.

The mountain rumbled, and Aki, one of the men, shrieked. He was sure the worst demons lived there. Ulf felt differently. He thought this place was too beautiful to be the home of demons. The home of spirits, maybe, but good ones unless they were angered.

"We cross the ice river!" Ulf declared, and the men looked at him questioningly. He was leading them to death and didn't care! Something in his eyes made them obey. They took the burdens from the three carts and tied them to the animal's backs. Ulf could see narrow passages and deep crevasses, and he knew he would have to leave his carrying logs behind.

Dog stepped onto the ice first, and Tabat was the second to bravely follow. This shamed the rest of the men into following without a murmur. The little goats were sure-footed, and the reindeer were nearly as stable. Puppy and Knife Tooth had the worst time. They crept low to the ground with their tails between their legs. Again, Dog and Tabat had to keep talking to them to put courage into their hearts. The men looked fearfully about them. The blue crevasses were so deep they couldn't see the bottom. The mountain was so high they could hardly see the top. Suddenly, it rumbled and shook, and a wide gorge opened up in front of them as if by magic! Trembling, they went around, knowing every minute that another might form right where they stood! The glacier was vast, and they hurried as fast as they could. Still, it took them two hours to cross. Dog wished they could stop and make feet-skins, but Ulf said no because stopping wasn't safe. When they were on land again, they wouldn't need feet-skins.

Being so high made the men dizzy and was bad magic, so they started downhill when they crossed the glacier. They soon reached timber country again and felt much better because the trees were not as big and terrifying as the bare glaciers. They were walking along a natural ledge that was wide in some places and narrow in others, but easy enough to travel. They began to think their troubles were over. The mountain rumbled again, and they could feel it shake! It was slight in its severity at first, but then it roared and heaved as though it was very angry with the men. A great tree crashed over a ledge and splintered into a pile of short logs and needles. The animals huddled together in a group and refused to move. Even the natural fear the little goats had of the wolves was conquered in the great common terror.

"Earthquake!" shrieked Dar, and the rest of the men began to howl.

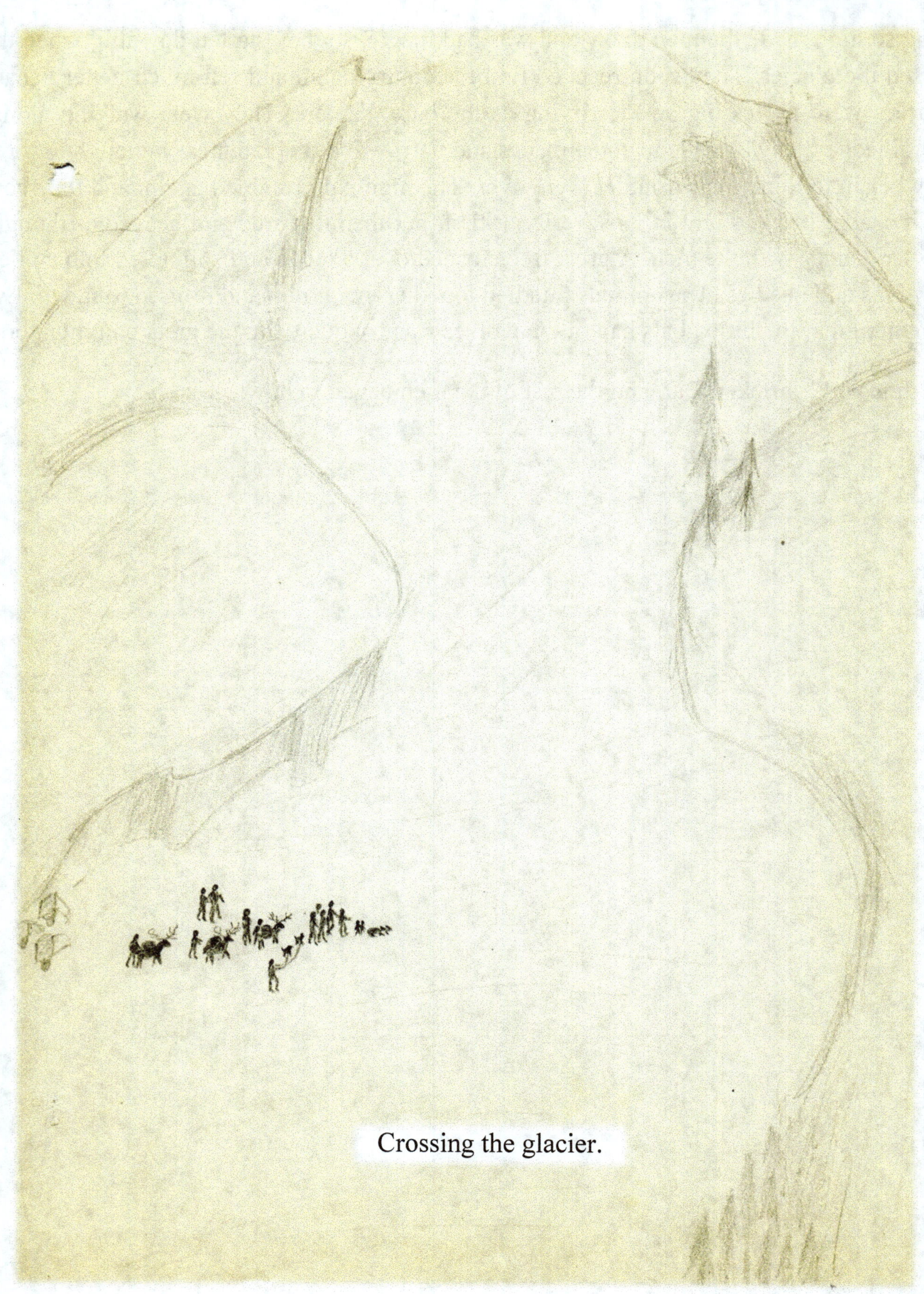

Crossing the glacier.

"Quiet!" shouted Ulf. "Crying won't stop the earthquake." The men were quiet, but they did not calm down. They had reckoned without the frequent shaking of the earth in this mountain country. Tabat heard a different rumble that seemed to come from above.

"Get back against the cliff!" Tabat yelled as he ran. The animals were already as close as they could be. The men pressed against the quivering wall of the earth–all that is, except one, and he was hit by one of the huge boulders Tabat had seen high above rolling downhill. The rock knocked the man backward, pushing him over the cliff. He didn't even have time to cry out. There were many boulders, rocks, and stones tearing down the mountainside. Some of them uprooted trees and sent them crashing down. The earth under the men's feet shook and trembled. They all expected the cliff above to fall on them or the ledge to give way at any minute. Dog had eaten a big breakfast that morning, and now he wished he hadn't. He had this awful feeling that he was going to be sick. He didn't know whether to hold his stomach or his mouth. The earth was shaking–no, it was whirling! Faster and faster-Tabat was upside down, and he had three faces! Fern caught Dog just as he was about to pitch over into the path of flying rocks.

Ulf didn't have time to worry about Dog, for suddenly, the ledge shook and ripped apart with the loudest noise yet! A small crack several feet from them slowly widened into a great crevasse! They were imprisoned on the mountain by a six-foot wide, thousand-foot-deep fall directly across the ledge!

Aki, the Reindeer man, suddenly ran to the edge of the crack and laughed. Then, before anyone could stop him, or even before he knew what he was doing, he jumped.

"He lost his mind," said Ulf. "You must not let yourselves go like that. Remember, we are not dead yet!" It seemed that with this great fissure, the mountain burned out its fury, and with a few last tremors, it again settled down to its old calm.

Dog didn't know whether to
hold his stomach or his mouth.

Ulf sighed with relief. At least this one danger was finished. He bent over Dog and patted his wrists and ankles. One of the men brought some of the salt water in his cupped hand. Gently he poured it down Dog's throat. The little boy sputtered and opened his eyes. The whirling had stopped, and there was Tabat, right side up and with only one face. That face was laughing.

"Come to, Dog. It's all over now. You are a baby."

"I'm not a baby. I am sick!"

"It's all right, Dog. How do you feel now?"

"I'm better now. What happened?"

"You fainted," said Ulf. "But come, we have to hurry and get across that crack. Some of you men go back along the ledge and bring me at least two fallen trees. Boys, you get as many thongs off the packs as you can. I have an idea." Now that the terrible earthquake was over, the men were brave again and quickly set about the tasks Ulf gave them.

They found three fallen trees on a wide part of the ledge and dragged them back to Ulf, who set to work chopping off the branches and cutting the trunks until they were about ten feet long. He tied those logs with the thongs, and at one end, he fastened long thongs, longer than the bridge.

"You, Fern, Root, and Pand, help me stand this on end the thongs are on up. I want it over at the edge of the crevasse. Yes. Steady. Now the rest of you hold the bottom so it won't slide. Fern, you take one thong. I'll take the other, and we will let the bridge over the crack easy so it won't bounce. Slow! Slow! Tabat, go over to Dog, he's still sick."

Dog was very ill. The salt water was just what he did not need, but of course, the men thought the medicine water was good for anything. Dog faintly heard the men cheering and Tabat shouting that the bridge was a success. Dog didn't even care. The demons were leaping around in his stomach, and all he wanted was to be left alone.

Ulf was the first to cross. When he found it safe, he led the frightened Puppy over. He then came back for Knife Tooth, the goats, and each reindeer. Lastly, he carried Dog over because he thought the great height might make him dizzy, and he'd faint again. Each man crossed the bridge safely, and once on the other side, they all had the feeling that the worst of the trip was over, barring calamities. A little farther along the ledge, they went under a waterfall, and Dog stuck his head into the cold, fresh deluge. After that, he felt normal again and sang bravely to prove he was really not a baby.

The ledge widened and tilted, and soon they were on a grassy slope. Short mountain flowers grew everywhere, and Dog and Tabat made wreaths for their hair and to put around the necks of the reindeer. Every once in a while, the men would swallow, and their ears would pop. Fern said it was the mountain demons leaving. It didn't take as long to go down the mountain as to climb up, and soon they were back in the forests of the foothills. They passed one place where there was a great patch of fruit trees, all in bloom. Ulf made up his mind to find that place where the fruits were ripe, but he didn't have the slightest idea where he was.

The next evening, they found a fire spout and camped by it all night. They said it was a hair from the sun mammoth that had fallen to the ground. In reality, it was a spout of gasses escaping from the earth, which had been ignited by a bolt of lightning.

For several more days, they traveled through the foothills, and Ulf was getting worried. He didn't want to go back through the mountains, but still, he didn't see how else he could find the village of Pang. He began to think of Sand and Sky and the little girl, and he was glad he had Dog with him. He could talk to Dog, and his son was the only one who knew they were lost.

One day they came to a place that seemed familiar to Dog, and Puppy sniffed around as though he also recognized the place. His fur bristled, and he was growling. The scar on his flank stood out the way it always did when he was angry. That scar reminded Dog.

"Father! Here is where Puppy killed the saber-toothed tiger! We are a half a day journey from home!" The men brightened up and broke into a half-run. As the trees became familiar, they laughed and shouted.

The women heard the cheers and saw Puppy and Knife Tooth running toward them, so excited they could hardly bark. The rest of the party soon arrived, and the wild beasts near Pang were frightened by the loud cheering that came from the village. It was a happy day. The exploring party had been given up for lost, and the spring had been long and lonesome for the ones who stayed behind. Sand scolded Dog for going and praised him for his bravery all at once. Then she turned to Ulf.

"You're thin, Ulf. I won't have you getting so thin. You must eat much food. I won't have you getting so thin!" Ulf and Dog let her feed them and wait on them. Oh, it was good to be back! The trip, on the whole, had been pleasant, but nothing was as nice as home.

It took many nights around the council fire to relate the adventures of the whole excursion. The boys envied Dog and Tabat, and the women worried about the earthquake, even though it was all over.

The two little goats and the reindeer were installed as village property, and Dar was given many presents to take home to his tribe. The tribe of Pang waved goodbye to Dar, and then returned back to its old routine. The expedition into the wild was over, and it had been good magic.

Chapter Nine:

Fire Again

Far to the north of the Reindeer tribe, Fire and his family lived peaceably enough. In the winter, they stole choice reindeer from the herdsmen's flocks. However, Fire was not happy. He knew Ulf and his tribe were living in comfort, and it made him very angry. When spring came, he began to plan how he could destroy Ulf, and he sent his sons out scouting. One day in late spring, his oldest son, Wide Eye, came home with the astounding news that Ulf had been away from the tribe for over a moon, but he had returned. When he heard this, Fire boxed Wide Eye's ears.

"Witless boy! Why didn't you find that out before? Our opportunity has come and gone. Oh, you empty head!" He chased poor Wide Eye into the cave and allowed him no dinner.

All that night, Fire stared into the flames and thought. *It might still be an opportune time to strike. Ulf would be tired and not alert. Yes, now all I have to figure out is how I would accomplish my end.* When morning came, Fire chuckled to himself. A plan had come to him, and it promised to work!

The pelts the men had gathered on their trip had been divided among them. The bags of salt water were given to Bearclaw because he was the medicine man, and it was medicine. He hung them on the walls of his cave beside the many strings of dried herbs and magic plants.

Puppy and Knife Tooth did nothing but rest for several days, and all the little cubs could not coax them to play. They seemed to say, "Go away. We have been places and seen things and have not time for such foolish goings on."

Ulf had completely forgotten his enemy to the north. He and Fern had been having many long talks with Bearclaw about the sea and the fruit trees, and the earthquake. Bearclaw said the spirits must surely be pleased, or else they would have destroyed them. This made Ulf very happy because he didn't like to think he had been the cause of any misfortune that might come to the tribe.

Sand was out with the women gathering herbs and digging roots to store away. She had the baby in a skin across her back. There were many things in the forest these people could eat, and it was the women's work to gather them. They formed a circle so no wild beast would catch them unaware. Sometimes, they sang funny little songs, and sometimes they talked about the women on the other side of the circle. Now that Fire's wife was gone, there were only a few that belonged to other tribes.

"Pig!" screamed one of the women, and almost as soon as she closed her mouth, the space was empty. All the women sprang for the lower branches and swung themselves into the trees. They were none too early, for the wild pig was a fast creature, and it charged into what had been the group of women. It looked around, baffled, and then began rooting around the fine pile of vegetables it found.

"My back aches," said Sand, "from digging roots for–pigs!" Two sows had come to join the boar, and they were having an excellent time. None of the women would come down for fear the boar would charge and gore them with his ugly tusks. "I wish Ulf would come," complained Sand.

Ulf, meanwhile, was in the cave with Dog and Sky. The two little boys were watching him tinker with a large flat stone and a pile of little ones. Occasionally, he would send the boys out to get some clay from the riverbank in a skin bag. He remembered how the boys built their snow fort and filled the chinks with more snow. He was building a small rock wall on each side of the indoor fire and filling the cracks with clay. When this was done, he rested the flat stones on the sides directly over the flames. The smoke then came out the front instead of going up the crack in the wall. The only thing left to do was make an opening. He removed the flat stone and chipped a rude semicircle out of the side that was pushed against the wall. When he replaced the stone, he was rewarded by seeing the smoke issue from the hole and sail merrily up the crack, which was really a natural chimney. Now Sand could put her meat and water in a bowl and set it on top of the hot rock, and it would boil with much less trouble. Ulf beamed with pleasure and pride. "I wish Sand would come home," he said.

Dog showed Jet the fine cooking stone, and little Sky said, "Tooking stove, Jet."

"Not stove, stone." Ulf corrected him, but Sky could only say stove. Jet wanted to try this idea, so she put some roots and water into a bowl and sat it on the so-called stove. Dog watched her. She was indeed very capable for such a little girl. The stone took a long time to warm up, and Ulf told them stories while they waited.

Back in the woods, Sand and the rest of the women were becoming more and more impatient. Sand was getting cramps from squatting on the limb of the tree, and she had never before realized how heavy the baby was. Nobody came near the place where the pigs rooted. Even Puppy and Knife Tooth were snoozing by the new cooking stone. A full hour later, the pigs had their fill and wandered off. The stiff women climbed out of the trees, gathered what was left of their food, and started home. Sand was angry. She thought Ulf should have come and chased the pigs away. She became angrier with every step nearer the cave, and when she heard Ulf and the children laughing, it was all she could do to keep from throwing the roots into the river.

"Look, Sand," said Ulf when he saw her.

The stiff women gathered what was left of their food.

She interrupted. "Look! Look at me! There I sat in a tree while the pigs ate our food, and what did you do? Did you come and kill the pigs? You didn't. You were telling stories!"

Fern was passing by, heard Sand, and laughed to himself. 'Ulf may be chief with the men, but at home, he is the same as any of us. His carved necklace doesn't mean a thing at home.'

"Wait Sand, wait," said Ulf. "How could I know there were pigs around? See what I made so you wouldn't have to carry hot rocks and burn your hands?"

"Stove! Stove!" shouted Sky.

Sand looked at the cooking stone and at the little bowl of roots cooking on top, and she smiled. She was not really angry, only tired from sitting in the tree for so long.

"Oh, I am lucky!" she exclaimed. "Ulf, you are the wisest man in Pang."

"Stove!" shouted Sky.

"Not stove, little rabbit, but stone," said Dog, but soon he, Jet, and everyone began to call the cooking stone a stove because little Sky could not say it any other way. It was then that the women who had not been so greedy or so fast were repaid. Those who'd had to take inferior caves with cracks in the walls were now the only ones who were able to keep indoor fires and have stoves.

Bearclaw went to the cave of Ulf that night and ate with them so he could see how much easier cooking was with their stove, and he pronounced it good magic. Bearclaw also came to ask when they were going to name the little girl. Several babies were in the village now, and it was time they had names. Dog wanted to call her Cry Baby because she was fretful. Sand didn't like that one bit. All Sky could think of to say was Stove, and, of course, that was no name for a baby. Ulf thought Twig would be best because her arms and legs were so thin. Sand was hurt. She knew the baby wasn't very healthy, but she didn't like to be reminded of it.

"You know, Sand," said Ulf, "twigs are very beautiful when they are older and have blossoms and leaves on them." Sand considered his words, and at last, she agreed. Twig was to be the little girl's name. Dog told Bearclaw the news, and he was happy. He thought now she might pick up because she had a name.

The old medicine man had made much magic over the little girl, and it hadn't helped. He had given her a tiny bit of salt water, but it seemed to make her sick. The people learned that while it was good for some things, it wasn't at all good for others. Perhaps it was a name Twig needed.

Fire and his older sons started out early one morning. It would take about four days to get down to the village of Pang. They carried long leather thongs and a few hides, and each knew exactly what to do. Fire had a bow and arrows. He shot birds and rabbits for them to eat on the way. He was very happy when he thought of how clever he was. They went around the Reindeer village because they knew that to be seen meant death. They passed the fire hole that was the regular camping place for the trading parties going between the two villages. By that point, they knew they were near Pang and would have to go carefully.

Finally, they reached the place where they were to stay. It was deep in a narrow gorge between two foothills. Trees had fallen over the top of it and were covered with vines. It was an excellent place to hide. Fire cut two long poles from a young tree. He trimmed all the branches off and skinned the bark.  When this was finished, he gathered a great pile of rocks into one of the pelts. By this time, it was night, but he didn't care. After cautioning his sons to stay there, he grinned, picked up the bag of stones, and started toward Pang.

Ulf awoke early the next morning and went to the entrance of the cave to get some fresh air. He noticed the birds, the clouds over the river, and the green fields on the other side before he noticed the strange trail of stones leading from his cave to the forest. These stones were not ordinary stones. They had been carefully laid a few feet apart, leading away. Ulf couldn't remember Dog making such a trail, but he wanted to be sure.

Dog, sleepy-eyed, told him he had not placed the stones. Sand wondered why he would think she did it, and Sky said it was more fun to build hills with rocks than to spread them around like that.

Dog ran into Jet's cave and grabbed her by the arm to wake her up. She hadn't seen the trail before. Ulf decided it must have been made by some spirit who wanted him to come to the forest. Sand was worried. She didn't want him to go out there all alone, but Ulf would not stay. After they had eaten, he started to follow the strange path.

The trail went up over the hills, across tiny stream, down into valleys, and often doubled back upon itself. It was very mysterious to Ulf, and the longer he followed it, the more determined he was to come to the end of it. Finally, the row of rocks led into a little gorge, almost completely covered with trees and vines. There it ended, and there stood Ulf, wondering what to do next.

He didn't have to wonder long. Suddenly, from above came a very effective lasso made of long sinews. It whirled over Ulf's head and tightened around his neck. He was held there, and Fire tied the thong to the fallen tree's trunk. Then he and his three sons stepped out of hiding and stood before Ulf. Ulf raised his bow, but another son behind him jerked his arm down and roughly grabbed the bow and all the arrows in his quiver. Ulf swung around and hit him, knocking him unconscious, but the effort jerked the thong around his neck, and he nearly choked to death.

"The wise Ulf is very foolish," said Fire. He tied each end of a thong around Ulf's wrists, leaving a length in the middle. "You see," he said, "Fire is very tired, and Ulf must carry him home!" He tied Ulf's ankles in the same way. "That is to keep you from running away." He laughed.

Ulf never spoke a word. He knew he could do nothing until the chance came. He watched the sons bring out a litter made of two long poles and a bearskin. They laid it on the ground, and Fire sat majestically upon it.

Ulf picked up the back end, and two of Fire's sons carried the front. Wide Eye carried his unconscious brother across his shoulders, and they started northward. Ulf thought he would find Fire's home now, and if he were quiet and waited his chance, he might change his luck.

At the end of the day, they stopped to eat, and Ulf was given a tiny piece of meat. Fire explained that he wouldn't have given him anything, but he must keep him strong enough to hold up his end of Fire's crude throne. They continued on again, and Ulf noted they kept off of the beaten trail. Fire and his sons sang gaily, and Ulf often joined them. He knew he could irritate Fire by appearing happy, and that was just what he did. It worked, and Fire seethed. Perhaps making him too angry wasn't good for Ulf, but he never thought of that.

All day Sand fretted, and Dog wondered what had become of Ulf. Finally, in the late afternoon, Dog decided to follow the trail himself. He took his bow and arrows and his pouch, which contained the flint and stone, his flint knife, and a thong. He told his mother and Jet not to worry, called Puppy, and started on the unusual, winding trail. It was nearly evening when he reached the end of it and found nothing. Puppy, however, was wiser. He found a smell. The hated scent of Fire was the strongest, and he bristled his fur and growled as he sniffed around the gorge. Then he found the scent of Ulf, and he wagged his tail. The two odors went along with several others that Puppy didn't know so well. Snout to the ground, Puppy started up the trail, which Fire had not reckoned on. Even if he had, he couldn't erase their scents.

 Dog understood Puppy's actions and ran along behind him. They stopped only long enough to shoot, cook, and eat a bird. Then, as it was night, Dog made a torch before he put his fire out, so they could keep right on going. Demons, same as animals, hated fire.

Ulf, Fire, and his sons also kept on the trail all night. Fire didn't want anyone else to sleep for fear that Ulf might, somehow, get away. However, he slept upon the litter as it was carried through the forest.

Dog forgot to be sleepy as he raced along the unseen trail with Puppy. The morning found him three-quarters of the way to the Reindeer village, as Ulf was being tossed a small piece of meat just a short distance west of that same village. Dog killed another bird, and he and Puppy ate it half raw. He didn't need his torch in the daytime, so he carefully put it out, and he and his wolf were on their way again. Fire laughed and bounced around on the litter, which made it very hard to carry. If it had not been for the watchful eyes of Wide Eye and Bub, who had come too, Ulf might have tossed away his end and made a run for it. As it was, he would just have to wait, even though he was growing very weary. By that night, they were up near the herds of reindeer, and Dog and Puppy were about halfway between them and the Reindeer village. Both parties stopped long enough to eat before spending another night walking.

The sons of Fire took turns carrying the litter, and there were two of them in front at a time. No one relieved Ulf, who carried his end alone. He wished Fire would let him ride, and yet, it was very lucky he didn't. Puppy was following Ulf's scent, and if it left off suddenly, Puppy would not be able to find him. It was really better for Ulf that Fire was so cruel.

The country was grassy, and the moon so bright that Dog didn't need a torch. He seemed to realize the need to be cautious. He and Puppy were both exhausted, but they kept up a sort of half-walk and half-trot that was fast but still did not fatigue them quite so much.

In the brilliant dawn, Fire reached his home. He jumped off the litter, and Ulf fainted. It was terrible for a strong man to do, but he was tired and had received almost no food. Fire's wife dragged him into the cave and poured water on him.

When he sputtered and sat up, she gave him something to eat. Then he went to sleep, and Fire let him rest before he told him what he was going to do. Fire's sons were sleepy too, and they flopped on their pelts and were asleep even before Ulf.

In the early afternoon, Dog and Puppy entered a woodsy glade and saw three young children playing in front of the cave. Dog told Puppy to be quiet, and he listened to their chatter. Soon he heard them speak of the chief of Pang, who was inside. Dog nodded to himself, and he and Puppy crept silently up behind the cave. Here they crawled under a vine-covered log, and they, too, slept.

Toward evening Ulf awoke and wondered where he was. When he saw Fire, he remembered.

"Ah, our guest awakes. And I suppose you would like to know what happens next?"

"Yes, if you don't mind." Ulf tried to appear unconcerned.

"Oh, I don't. Not one bit. You, my friend, are to remain alive, and do all of our work. The harder or lower the task, the quicker we shall give it to you. How do you like that?"

"Fire does not think. He does not know, perhaps, that I will get away the first chance I have. It would be much better to kill me at once."

"Fire does think. The mighty Ulf will have no chance. In the daytime, he will have a guard, and at night he shall be securely tied to that tree outside. The cave is too good for him. Never shall those wrist and ankle thongs be removed, and the cave of Fire is well hidden. No one shall find you here."

But Fire was wrong again. Dog, just outside the cave, heard them through the smoke hole. Fire's wife had seen the crack in Sand's cave and had dug one for Fire in his. It was lucky for Ulf that she did, for Dog heard every word.

Dog and Puppy on the trail.

Ulf laughed. "Your thongs are too long. I can untie them."

"No. In the daytime, your guard will prevent you, and at night you shall be tied much too well to reach them."

Dog laughed to himself, as he felt the outline of his flint knife in his pouch. Soon it would be night. He had to hold Puppy and keep telling him to be quiet to prevent him from roaring at that hated voice. Dog knew that if he let Puppy go in there, his pet would be a target for the arrows of Fire and his sons. The sun painted the sky red and purple, and it seemed to Dog that it would never turn blue and get dark. He saw Fire tie Ulf to the tree, and he felt like sending an arrow through him then and there. Fire went into his cave, but Dog waited until it was very dark, and he could hear the people inside snoring.

He told Puppy to lie down and be quiet and crept toward Ulf. Ulf saw him and opened his mouth, but Dog put one finger to his lips. Ulf was astounded when he recognized him. Swiftly Dog cut his father's bonds, and when Ulf was free, he hugged Dog for a minute, but never spoke a word.

"Puppy," Dog whispered, and when the big animal came out of hiding, the three ran downstream as fast as they could go. They had not come up the stream because it ran beside the Reindeer village, but now the idea was speed. They wanted to reach the caves of their friends as soon as possible. Ulf asked Dog no questions. That could wait until they were safe. All night they ran, and when morning came, they were nearly at the Reindeer village.

When morning came to the cave of Fire, he went outside to laugh at Ulf and found him gone! He roared in anger. He called his family and yelled at them for having been asleep. He boxed his wife's ears and sent her scurrying to the cave. Then he and the same four sons started downstream. He knew that Ulf and his rescuer would never go inland. He ran at a pace that he had never run before. His anger made his legs go faster and faster until his sons were left far behind.

Dog, Ulf, and Puppy ran into the Reindeer village and threw themselves onto pelts in the nearest cave. They were exhausted, but they were safe. Fire would never venture into the village, and Ulf knew a band of his men was up here on a trading trip. They could all return together. He told his story to Dar, and Dog added his part. Puppy was the big hero of the day. He got more pets and praise than he had ever had before. He grinned and lolled his big tongue out of the side of his mouth. He heard his name being repeated many times, and he loved it. He hated when he was neglected a little the next day as they started back to Pang.

The whole village of Pang turned out to meet them. The story was told again, and Puppy was again the center of attraction. The people had heard the story of the trail of stones from Sand, and they had feared greatly for their chief. Now Ulf was home, due to Dog and Puppy, and he presented to Dog a finer flint knife than he had ever owned before. Around Puppy's neck, he placed a collar made of a skin with all the fur plucked off. Sand had taken a sharp tool and pressed pictures of Puppy's exploits in the soft leather. Thus, the two heroes were rewarded, but Puppy liked his big dinner even better than the collar.

Far to the north, Fire and his sons returned home empty-handed. For days Fire sat chewing his knuckles. Ulf had escaped! Truly, the spirits of good fortune must travel with this man!

Chapter Ten:

Newcomers

Dog and Jet were standing in the river. Both carried clay bowls tied with thongs over their shoulders. Into these, they tossed the wriggling fish. The sun was bright, and all of Dog's freckles were blossoming forth in great style. Jet teased him about them. Her freckles were just on her nose and under her eyes. On a fine day, Dog's freckles covered his entire face. They were laughing and bantering with each other when Tabat came running down to them. He was very excited.

"Look! Up the river!" he exclaimed and pointed. Dog and Jet looked and gasped. Down toward Pang came many large boats filled with people! The children had never seen such a thing before. The men had long poles to guide the boats. Through the rough parts, only one pole would be lifted at a time in a sort of walking motion. The rest kept the boats from being dashed to pieces on a rock. In the front of the first boat stood a woman holding a leafy branch, the sign of peace. Dog had no branch, so he held up one of the fish from his bowl as his peace offering. As the son of the chief, he felt it was his place to welcome these obviously friendly people. Jet ran up to tell the tribe of Pang as the boats came to the shore.

Suddenly one of the women shrieked, "Wolf!" They hastily scrambled back into the boats. Puppy had come gamboling down to the river to coax Dog to play!

"Back Puppy," said Dog. "Go home." And as Puppy obediently trotted back, Dog told the amazed people that the wolves were tame and would not hurt them. However, they were dubious and even more alarmed when Ulf and the rest of the people came to the shore with all of the dogs playing around them.

Ulf stepped forward. "Who is your chief?"

A man arose. "Our chief is dead, but I will speak for these people. I am Yab."

"What is your tribe?"

"We are what is left of the Arrow tribe."

"Where do you come from?"

"From far up the river in the Long Winter countries."

"Why did you leave?"

"Our home was invaded by a fierce people. They killed many of us, and the rest they made slaves. We built these dugouts, and one night we made our escape down the river. For many, many weary days, we have traveled, looking for a new home."

Ulf studied the people carefully. They were not as large as the men of Pang and were not stocky, like the Reindeer men. They had light yellow hair and fair skins, and looked like good people. After a short conference with Bearclaw, Ulf raised his hand.

"Your search is ended. If Yab, as your leader, will mix his blood with mine, and you all will accept me as your chief, then you may settle here as a new part of the tribe of Pang. Here you will find some empty caves. We never have a food shortage, and we are protected by the river and the hills. Our village is pleasant. Do not be afraid of the wolves. They have been changed into a different breed of animal called the dog, after my son, who tamed them. They will not hurt you. Will you stay?"

The people chattered amongst themselves for a short length of time, and then Yab turned to Ulf. "We will stay and join your tribe. We will accept you as our chief, and will fight for you."

Yab gave the signal, and the people again disembarked. There were not enough empty caves for all of them, so some families had to move in with others until new caves were dug. There were many children, and they all grouped together at one end of the glade and stared at the children of Pang, who were at the other end of the glade, staring back at them.

One of the little blonde girls tripped and fell over a rock on the way to join her friends. Tabat ran and picked her up. She smiled.

"Snow," she said, pointing at herself.

"Tabat," he answered, and they were friends immediately. Soon, the others began to mingle, and when Dog suggested they go swimming, they all laughed and followed him. The water was cold in the North Country, and the blonde children could not swim. They were surprised to find the same river was so much warmer down here. It didn't take long for them to learn to paddle around, and Dog told them that they'd surely be able to swim by the end of the summer.

Tabat brought Snow over to Jet, and the two little girls looked shyly at each other. They were both about the same size, and Tabat thought they should be friends.

Jet said, "I will give you one of my wolf cubs, only they are dogs now. Don't be afraid." The little girl looked alarmed at the idea.

"Yes," she replied, knowing that if Jet wasn't afraid, she shouldn't be. "I will give you a white pelt like this. It is from the great northern bear that comes down to our land in the winter." The two little girls, with their friendship established, ran into the water to watch Dog and Tabat, who were showing off outrageously to the new children.

The boys were in the middle of the river, where it was deep. They turned somersaults in the water and raced with much splash and churn. They laid on their backs and spouted water through their mouths. Jet could hold herself back no longer. She swam out and challenged Dog to a race. Tabat was to be their starter. They stood on the shore until he shouted, then they ran into the water and swam pell-mell to the other side. The children yelled and cheered; some for Jet, while others for Dog. They both finished together, laughing and sputtering. They ran out of the water, up to shore, then turned, dove back in, and were off again. Again, they finished at a dead heat. They tossed their bright red hair out of their eyes and sat on the ground to rest. It had been such fun!

Snow went over to Tabat. "Will you show me how to do that?" she asked shyly.

Tabat grinned. It would be easy to teach her to swim. They went out as far as she was able to stand up, and Tabat pushed her over on her face. Instinctively, she splashed out and swam. When they got onto the shore, she hit Tabat on the chest.

"You horrid, hateful, terrible boy!" she cried.

"But you swam! That's the way to learn!"

"Oh, did I? Is it? I forgive you then." She stopped hitting him and ran back into the water. "Do it again!" she called. Very soon, all of the new children were being roughly pushed into the water by the children of Pang. Of course, they didn't tell the newcomers that they had learned to swim only a short time before.

 When they tired of this new sport, the new children became acquainted with the tame wolf pack. They were a little timid at first, but when the dogs smelled them and didn't even attempt to bite, they patted them gingerly. Jet brought Bite over to Snow.

They both finished together.

"His name is Bite, but he does it easy and wouldn't hurt you for anything. You may have him."

Snow stroked Bite's ear, and he licked her arm. She shrank back in alarm when his tongue first touched her, but she smiled as soon as she saw he meant no harm.

With their pets at their heels, the whole flock started to make the rounds of the village and surrounding country. Dog was the spokesman, and he showed the blonde boys and girls the best trails, the prettiest glades, and the highest trees. When evening came, every child was glad to go home to eat and rest. It had been a long, exciting day.

That night there was to be a great ceremony to welcome the northern people into the tribe of Pang. As soon as the moon came up, everyone began to gather in the glade. A huge council fire was lit with a ceremonial prayer from Bearclaw. When the flames were leaping high into the air, the medicine man rose and called for Ulf and Yab to come forward. Dog noted with pride that Ulf was at least a head taller than Yab. Bearclaw brought out a little wooden dish he had carved himself for the occasion. He then took out his flint knife and cut Ulf's hand. Ulf let a drop of blood run into the dish. Next, it was Yab's turn, and he, too, let a drop of blood run into the dish, mingling with that of Ulf's. Bearclaw held the dish over the flames.

"Oh, spirit of the fire! You are the spirit that watches over the men of Pang. We have brought into the tribe more men. Watch over them, too! To show that they are now true men of Pang, we offer you a drop of their blood, mingled with a drop of the blood of our chief. Henceforth these men shall live with us, hunt with us, and fight with us. We shall all be one as the mighty tribe of Pang!"

With these words, Bearclaw placed the dish on the coals, and as it burned, all the warriors danced around the fire. It was during the dancing that the new boys became a little envious of Dog and his friends, for the boys of Pang had taken part in a battle and had a right now to dance the fighters' dance. Dog and Tabat howled very ferociously when they danced past Jet and Snow, and when they passed their mothers, they made hideous faces and nearly frightened the women to death. The two were very proud of themselves.

When the fighters' dance was over, everyone rose and danced around the fire. This was the torchlight dance, and at the end of it, the men lit the way to their family's home. Soon only Bearclaw was left, and he smiled with satisfaction. He felt these new colonists would be a credit to Pang, and he was glad. Tomorrow, he would have to investigate those strange hollow logs they had arrived in.

Dog had long been regarded as the leader of the boys. When they thought he had the head sickness, they turned for a time to Tabat. But as soon as it was discovered they were wrong, they again accepted Dog. He was the son of the chief, and besides, he always thought of the best games and knew where the best places were. Dog naturally took command of the newcomers, and Shal didn't like that one bit. Shal had always been the captain of the fair-haired boys, and he resented Dog casually stepping into his position. He would much rather step into Dog's. Dog knew Shal didn't like him, and he knew he would have to fight him so he could remain the leader. He discussed this with Tabat, who promised to help, but Dog knew he'd have to do it alone.

The morning was bright and cheerful, but there was tension in the air. The children stayed in their caves and only peeked out. Finally, Dog issued from his cave and strode slowly toward the glen. Near the other end of the village, Shal also came from his cave and walked toward the glen. The other children followed after them, one by one, but remained well behind the two boys. They were anxious to see the outcome of this feud. Even little Sky trotted along beside Tabat with a very serious look on his face.

The two boys met in the center of the glade. They stood and looked at each other for a moment without speaking. Then they each shouted.

"Rabbit!" said Shal.

"Hyena!" said Dog.

Now Dog was on top, pounding Shal.

In an instant, the boys were at each other, hitting, biting, and clawing. Now Dog was on top, pounding Shal. Suddenly Shal turned, throwing Dog off balance. Shal was on top, pummeling Dog. He hit him in the nose, and Dog felt warm blood trickling down his lip. The boys from the north cheered. Shal had drawn first blood! This made Dog very angry. His red hair bristled almost like Puppy's, and his eyes squinted up with rage. The boys were on their feet and exchanging blows. Then Shal tripped Dog, and they were rolling on the ground again. Shal's eye had a funny, puffy look where one of Dog's fists had landed. Both had enough black and blue marks for six boys. Neither was winning, and neither was losing. Neither was up nor down. Back and forth across the glade, they raged. Shal was beginning to feel tired, but Dog wasn't. He was wiry, and it took a lot to tire him. He began to get the upper hand a bit, and the Pang boys felt cheered.

Suddenly, Dog's friends were amazed. Dog's arms dropped. He put his hand to his forehead and began to retreat. Then Tabat saw the reason why. Shal's thumb was pushed firmly in the hollow at the base of Dog's neck! That wasn't clean fighting, and Tabat sent up a howl. He raced out and hit Shal, who turned to face his new assailant. As soon as the thumb was released, Dog gulped and jumped on Shal's back, tumbling himself, Shal, and Tabat over in a heap. That was a signal that brought every boy in the glade into the fray. It turned into a great free-for-all. Even Sky lurked on the sidelines and pulled any locks of blonde hair he could reach.

The noises disturbed Bearclaw, who ran down to the glade and strode into the tangle of boys. He quickly singled out Dog and Shal and separated them.

"Stop!" he shouted, and the boys looked at him sheepishly. "What is this about?" They all began to jabber at once. Bearclaw turned to Fox Ear. "Tell me," he instructed the boy.

Fox Ear gulped. "They were seeing who was going to be the leader, and they were fighting it out themselves when Tabat saw Shal push Dog's neck with his thumb!" At this remark, even the fair-haired children looked scornfully at Shal, who was blushing with shame. "Then we all got into it!" finished Fox Ear.

Bearclaw stroked his beard. "Is this true, Shal?"

"Yes, I'm sorry. Dog is the real leader."

Bearclaw smiled and turned to the rest. "Do you all accept Dog as your leader? Will you all be as brothers now and stop this foolish fighting?" The children shouted in agreement, and Bearclaw was satisfied. "Dog, do you forgive Shal?"

"Yes, he is a good fighter." Dog smiled, and the blood that was caked on his lip cracked. Shal went up to him, and they each put their hands on the other's shoulders in the sign of peace.

"You all belong to the tribe of Pang now. Go and stand together." With these words, Bearclaw left the bruised and battered boys. They all grinned at each other, and then Dog turned and limped home. He had scraped his knee on a stone, and one of his ears tingled. His face was puffed up, bruised, and covered with blood from his nose. Besides that, he had been rolling in the dirt and was all muddy.

"Dog! Whatever happened to you?" exclaimed Sand when she saw him.

"I'm the leader!" he grinned, and Sand nearly fainted when she saw through his swollen lips that a tiny corner had been broken off of one of his front teeth!

"You go right down to the river and swim around until all that mud and blood is washed off. Leader or no leader, you look terrible!"

Dog laughed and ran to the river. He found he was not alone, for every boy that had been in the fight was there, sent by mothers' orders!

Ulf, Bearclaw, and Yab were discussing the problem of caves for the new families. Many were still living with others, and suitable places to dig caves were scarce. Bearclaw was staring at his little stove when slowly his eyes brightened, and he smiled.

"I know. If we can't dig them, we can build them!"

"How?" asked Yab and Ulf together.

"Look, we can take stones like our stoves were made and pile them high and round. Over the top, we can put branches of trees and cover them with the long, tough grass that grows up in the plains."

Yab jumped up. "Ho! We are lucky to join a tribe with such a wise medicine man! We will send the boys up to the plain country to get the grass!"

Work was begun almost at once. Bearclaw drew circles in the ground where the huts were to be built, and the men gathered huge piles of stone. The women were the mud carriers, and the children started on their several days' journey to the plains.

Dog and Tabat led the way because they had been there before. This time was different, however. Then it had been frosty and windy. Now the air was warm and the breeze gentle. They found the remains of their campfire between the log and the boulder. Here the children camped the first night and had a great time. They had a ceremonial fire and dance, all by themselves. Shal acted as the medicine man with a headdress he made out of leaves for the occasion. They danced and sang in a fine imitation of the adults. When they finally went to sleep, they were very tired boys.

Sky, who thought he was grown up because he was allowed to go on this trip, awoke before the others the next morning. He couldn't quite remember, at first, where he was. Then he saw the rest of the boys slumbering around him. He just sat there for a while, looking at the bright sky. The new sun cast long bars of brilliance through the trees, and the clouds were all pink and gold. Sky was glad he had been named after such a beautiful thing. He listened to the birds sing. They must have felt just as he did! He jumped up, ran over to his brother, and shook him.

"Morning, Dog, morning!" he shouted.

His cries awoke everyone, and soon the whole group was breakfasting on some early berries that grew nearby. They marched on. Late that afternoon, they planned to reach the plains. They laughed and sang on the way, and it made the trip seem much shorter. Before they even realized it, they had their flint knives out and were cutting the long, tough grasses.

All afternoon they cut, and in the evening, their backs were sore from bending. They were glad to light their campfire and eat the eggs of field birds. They were even glad to stretch out on the ground and go to sleep.

The next day they were hard at work again. Their knives were short, and they couldn't cut many grasses at a time. Still, slowly the bundles grew until they had enough. Then each boy took his own bundle and tied it up with thongs. They made a sort of harness to slip their arms through, so they could carry the grass on their backs. Dog made a little one for Sky, who ran from one to the other so they could all see he was doing his share.

Back toward Pang, they trotted, and met a group of men in the hills who were cutting slender, tough branches from trees. They wanted the kind that would bend without breaking. The boys camped that night with the men and helped them. On the morrow, they could all go home together.

The men had the reindeer and carrying boards to pile their burdens on, so they made good time. They arrived in Pang soon enough to help finish the huts.

The people encountered difficulty when they approached the top of the doorways. There was nothing to rest the stones on up there. They puzzled about this until Yab put a piece of wood, which was chiseled flat on both sides, on the layer of rocks. This board went over the place that was to be the top of the doorway. The next layer of rocks went from one end of the wood to the other, and all the remaining rows rested on the wood. It was so simple even Bearclaw was amazed.

In the center of each hut, there stood a tall, forked pole. The branches were tied firmly on the fork, and the other end of the branches rested on the edge of the wall. The women knew that wouldn't be enough, so they tied thinner branches that would bend around clockwise. Then these they fastened to the grasses. The little girls had separated the big bundles, making many small bundles ready to be attached to the branches. Right at the edge of the roof, they left a hole so they could have stoves. When these were made, the new huts were finished, and the people had a great feast in celebration of the event. To these people, the huts were the height of luxury and the very best magic, as well! Dog thought it gave the village a distinctive, if rather crowded, look.

He was glad to move the family that stayed with them someplace else. The newcomers were fine, and a credit to Pang and all that, yet, Dog was happy the first night the family of Ulf found itself alone. He lay on the pile of furs he shared with Sky and watched the outdoor fire flicker in the cave entrance. The flames grew blurry and indistinct, and soon Dog was asleep.

Chapter Eleven:

Baskets, Bison, and a Battle

The men of Pang were growing restless. The trading trips had stopped, because the Reindeer men wouldn't kill any of their animals in the seasons when hunting was good. In this way, they kept the herds from dying out. The lack of reindeer meat didn't bother the Pang people. Every time the hunters went out, they returned with food. The women dried some, tanned the hides, and made implements with the bones. They were always busy, but the men were doing nothing when they weren't out hunting.

A little time was lifted from their hands when the people from the north showed the Pang men their knives and other stone tools. They were not chipped, but polished! This was a significant improvement, for they were sharper and not full of rough jags. The northern men gladly showed Ulf and his tribe the art of polishing stone. They felt it was a fair price to pay for their new homes. For many days the men of Pang sat with all their stone tools, and soon not a chipped tool could be found in all of Pang! The other men had polished stone for as long as they could remember.

When this great task was finished, the men again became restless, and even the boys couldn't think of much to do. They swam, raced, and went berry picking, but still, time seemed to drag. And when time dragged on, boys became naughty.

When time dragged for little girls, they brought out their dolls and played family. The boys used to tease them down by the riverbank where they gathered.

"Silly girls! Silly play!" they would shout, make faces at the girls and trample down all the little caves they'd dug in the clay bank. Then the girls would go home in tears, and the small boys would get spanked. The big boys, though, were too much for their mothers, so they escaped punishment. Even Dog took part in the unmanly play. All the boys thought it was very clever.

One day Jet called Dog over to one end of the glen. There, beside a small bundle of plain grass, she sat down and motioned for Dog to do likewise.

"Dog, I don't like you when you spoil our doll caves and then laugh!"

"Aw, dolls are silly."

"Well, so are old spears and bows and arrows."

"What about the arrow I gave you?"

"That is the silliest one of all!"

"Why should I listen to you, you're only a girl!"

"You've got to listen. Sit!" Jet proceeded to lecture him on how grown-up men didn't act like that. She talked long and forcibly and made him sit up straight when Dog pretended to go to sleep. Dog grinned at her. She hated to be grinned at. She decided not to look at him, so she picked up the grass and played with it while she scolded. She pretended she was sewing and pulled the long strands in and out of each other. Dog noticed the unusual, haphazard mat that had formed in her hands.

They would make faces at the girls, and run up and trample all of the little caves they dug in the clay bank.

"Jet!" Dog interrupted. He hadn't been listening anyhow. "Look what you have. You could carry berries on that!"

Jet was too surprised to be angry at his inattention. They studied the little mat and figured if they laid the first grasses in a row and pushed the others in and out, it would be much tighter. They followed words with action and soon had a square woven mat! Jet was overjoyed and began to think of other ways to make them. She laid some in a circle and wove the others in toward the center. That didn't work so well, so Dog laid the ones that came out from the center first and wove the others around it.

That method would have worked all right, except the straight grasses weren't strong enough to hold the ones that were to curve around. Dog and Jet had found something to interest them now, and they worked hard. Dog cut many of the long, tough, yet slender branches that grew on willow trees. He laid these across each other, stretching them from the center to the outer edge. He found a thin piece of sinew in his pouch, and with that, he tied the branches together. Round and round, he wove the long grasses. But he would invariably disturb one of the twigs as he moved. Jet took all the ends, bent them up, and tied them together to keep them out of Dog's way.

They wove the grass strong and tight, and when it ran out, they wove in a couple of rows of willow branches to make it compact. Dog cut the long ends, and they expected the thing to spring back and lay flat. It didn't. The ends still pointed skyward, and the mat was shaped like a clay bowl!

"Why Dog, it's even better!" exclaimed Jet. They picked up the basket, for that's what it was, and carried it to Bearclaw. He said it was good magic and gave it to Jet. She showed it to her mother, who gave instructions in weaving to all the women. Jet told the people it was really Dog's discovery, and he beamed with pride when he saw the many uses they had for baskets.

Sand made a big one entirely of willow branches and hung it by thongs to the crossbar of something that looked very much like a barbecue spit. She lined the baskets with the softest pelts she had and made a cradle for little Twig to sleep!

When Dog and Jet went fishing, they put their fish in baskets instead of clay bowls. The bowl Puppy used to eat his dinner sat in a basket to keep it from breaking when he knocked it over. The women carried baskets on their backs when they were digging to throw the roots into. Now pigs might come, but they would spoil no more meals!

Soon, though, even this new excitement died down. Baskets became an everyday matter. The men wanted to go hunt again, but this time they promised to stay closer to home. They also promised to take all the bigger boys with them. This was to be a bison hunt in the plains to the sunset of the creek. They were to take no reindeer, but Puppy and his wolf pack were to go along.

Only a few men were left in Pang for protection. All the rest and the big boys started early in the morning. They sang a song about bison. Each man would sing his own verse, and then they would all shout, "Hi Yo! Hi Yo! The bison!" That was the closest thing they had to an actual song. The people left behind heard the happy tune fade in the distance.

The hunters went across the hills and met nearly all of the Reindeer men and boys when they arrived at the stream. Hunting bison was a new thing to them, and they were eager to get started. On the other side of the creek was a seemingly endless plain. There, roaming wide, they *the hunters* knew they would find bison.

Dog had never been on this side of the valley before, and he was thrilled. As he trotted along, he imagined his arrow killing the leader of the herd. He imagined himself planning the method of attack. It was a brilliant plot, but it had one difficulty. He planned for all the hunters to get into trees and drop upon the backs of bison as they passed by underneath. The difficulty was that there were no trees!

"What is in your head, Dog?" asked Tabat when Dog hadn't spoken for several minutes.

"There are no trees!" answered Dog sadly, and Tabat looked at him in alarm, but he said nothing.

Shal suddenly sent up a great cry. He saw bison and shouted as loud as he could. All the men heard him and looked in the direction he pointed. The worst thing was the bison also heard him, and the animals turned and ran away. Shal's father cuffed his ears, but Bearclaw said to let the boy alone. It was a mistake, and there would be other bison. This blunder brought out one necessity, however. The men had no set signal to use when one of them saw an animal. Bearclaw said he should stand still and point at the beast. That seemed like a good signal, so they proceeded across the plain with that difficulty out of the way.

The next bison herd was small, but the leader was a particularly large and hairy specimen. He had lowered his head and was swinging it from side to side when he smelled a new and strange scent. The men were all ready for the charge when an astonishing thing happened.

Wolves were usually murderous and cruel beasts, but they also had many instincts that were submerged and hidden. Taming the wolves and changing them to dogs had reversed the order. The cruelty and desire to kill became hidden, and loyalty and the desire to serve men emerged. Puppy and his band knew that, for some reason, the men wanted these ungainly and stupid beasts.

Instinctively, the wolves raced from the men and toward the herd. The bison were surprised and started to break away and run. The dogs chased them and forced them back to their leader by nipping at their heels. Having kept the herd intact, the dogs simply ran around it to keep any more bison from running away. Herding animals was something the wolves had never been taught. It was contrary to their wolf nature to refrain from the kill. The only explanation was that the knowledge of herding had always been there, waiting until the wolf became the dog before it showed itself.

The men were astonished. "Look!" exclaimed Fern. "We can bring the bison back and keep them in the small plain close to Pang!"

But Bearclaw saw an objection. "As soon as the dogs go home, the bison would run away. They are not as easily made content as the reindeer and goats. We must kill these beasts and take meat home." The men nodded. Bearclaw, as usual, was right.

Puppy saw Dog watching him. He looked at Dog and barked, wagging his tail. His mouth was open in the big foolish grin of the dog that had done something for which he wanted praise.

It was an easy matter for the men to slaughter the thirty-odd bison. The animals were so befuddled; they didn't know what was happening. The men struggled for a while when the wounds stung the animals but did not kill them. The men walked right into the midst of the herd with their great war axes. The men with bows and arrows ran around the fringe and shot into the herd. They were good shots and never hit any of the other men.

The bison were roaring with pain and fury, but there were too many enemies for them to do anything but stand in a huddled knot and sway their heads. When the animals were all dead, the people and dogs sat on the ground and rested. Later they would have a feast and then head home.

They built a fine fire and roasted the big leader. He wasn't very tender, but they were used to tough meat, and their teeth were strong. The men ripped the meat apart and carelessly tossed the bones to the dogs. The boys watched studiously, and when they finished their chunks of meat, they, too, tossed the bones over their shoulders with a very careful carelessness. They were hunters now and should act like hunters. Dog felt inches taller than he really was. He picked out fine bits of meat and threw them to Puppy, who was the happiest animal in the world. He loved Dog's praise more than anything, and Dog was not stingy with it.

The rest of the bison were cut up and tied with the same harness arrangement the boys had used to carry the grass for the huts. Jubilant, the men of Pang and the Reindeer clan prepared to start home. They were putting their burdens on their backs when, suddenly, one of the men pitched forward with a short, dark arrow in his back!

Yab saw the arrow and recognized it. "Enemies!" he said, but they could see no one. There was a sort of gulch nearby, and they investigated it, but there were no enemy tribesmen there. It was very mysterious!

Ulf shook his head. There was no use waiting. Again, they started across the plain. A Reindeer man was the next to fall with another of the strange arrows in the back of his neck. Nowhere could the men see anything but the tall plain grass. Then Ulf noticed a very significant fact. When the men fell, they were entirely hidden by the grass!

The men and the boys planned quietly. They didn't want their enemies to know that they had guessed where they were hidden. Suddenly, all at once, the Pang and Reindeer men turned with bows and arrows ready and shot into the grass away from them. It was a blind guess, but it worked! The quick barrage was answered by several screeches, and the enemy tribesmen jumped up and attacked!

The enemy was on three sides of the Pang men. Howling and screaming, they ran around them, shooting into their midst. The tribe of Pang would not idly let itself be killed! Dog had a great idea. He put a harness on backward, so the huge chunk of meat would be in front! He was glad, for almost at once, he saw a short arrow quivering in the section of bison! Ulf saw the idea, and soon every man and boy had their burdens on backward.

It was a desperate situation, and much as Ulf hated to risk the possibility of the dogs reverting back to wolves, he had to say, "Puppy! Dogs! Go get them!" At these words, the eager wolves sprang at the invaders, several of whom ran away in fright.

The Pang men plucked the arrows from their strange shields and used them right back. Fox Ear saw his Sunshine hit by an arrow, making him want to cry. Instead, he set his jaw and had the small satisfaction of seeing the man who killed the dog go down under an arrow shot by its master–himself. Because of the lucky bison meat, comparatively few Pang men were killed. They, in turn, killed many of their enemies, but it seemed their numbers were endless. The main danger facing the people was an arrow shortage. It was strange to see these men plucking the arrows out of their wounds and sending them back as calmly as though they were picking berries!

This was Dog's second battle, but it was his first where he was right in the middle of it. He was dreadfully frightened, but he wanted to look brave. He took his place in the circle of men and watched Ulf's face. When Ulf looked grim, Dog looked grim. When Ulf smiled, Dog smiled; though his was rather forced. He looked at Tabat, who was actually singing! Dog grinned at him, and he grinned back. But their arms never stopped pumping arrows into the yelling horde. They were rather clumsy with the big chunks of meat on their chests, but they did all right.

The invading tribesmen continued to dance around the group of hunters. Suddenly, one particularly ferocious man, who was all tattooed and decked with feathers, fell with an arrow from the bow of Bearclaw in his chest. He was their leader, and when he was killed, the rest scattered and fled; none too soon, for arrows were growing very scarce to the men of Pang.

"They will not come back," said Bearclaw, and again the Northern men were glad they had joined forces with the tribe of Pang!

The wolves chased the enemy tribesmen for a short distance, and then they came back to their masters. Bearclaw's Loyal and Fox Ear's Sunshine were dead. The rest were wounded, but not seriously.

Tabat had an arrow on his arm, but he laughed and said he was too well-padded to be hurt. Dog had been hit in the face with a stone and had a large purple welt on his cheek. The stone had been thrown by a new weapon. Dog picked the new weapon up and examined it. There were two thongs tied to a round piece of leather. In this piece, they placed a rock and whirled it around their heads by the thongs. It threw rocks with much more force than their arms. Dog found a stone and tried it out. Soon all the boys were forging among the dead, looking for slingshots, or throwing-thongs as they called them. They would be excellent for killing small animals.

The Pang and Reindeer warriors picked up their dead and wounded and started again. They would build a cairn over the dead as soon as they reached a rocky country. They could not leave them out in the plain, or the demons would get them, and they would never reach the land of the spirits. The going was slow, and it seemed to Dog that they would never arrive at the stream. They did, however, and there they found as many rocks as they could possibly want.

Here they stopped and laid the dead bodies in a row with their weapons and some of the bison meat beside them. They built the funeral fire and danced the solemn dance reserved for the burial of those who died in battle. Bearclaw sent their spirits into the spirit world with a very long prayer. When these honors were completed, they built the cairn. The boys felt very sad because one of their numbers, Feather, was laying in that row. It would be strange not to have him around, but then he had died as a warrior, and so was assured of good hunting in the spirit world.

Here, they and the Reindeer tribe separated, and soon they were in the hills nearing Pang. Dog was thinking how surprised the people would be when they learned that instead of merely hunting bison, they had also repulsed a horde of savage invaders!

The people were surprised, and many mothers vowed they would never again let their boys go on a hunt so far away from home. It seemed that something unlooked for always happened. The battle accomplished one good thing besides driving away the invaders--it put the new boys on the same footing as the old ones. They could all dance the fighter's dance now!

When Dog went home, Sky came running out to meet him. Sky had been lonely for his brother, and set up a joyful clamor when he saw him. Dog was home! Dog felt very brave and quite grown up. In fact, he felt old. His eleven years weighed heavily on his battle-scarred shoulders.

He didn't feel so old when Sand saw him. She looked at him critically. She turned him around and studied him from all sides. Dog was sure she must have been admiring his muscles. He swelled his chest and thrust out his chin. Why, he was nearly as tall as Sand! Sand studied him, and then she spoke. "Go down to the river and swim until you get yourself clean," she said.

Chapter Twelve:

Good Magic

Sand looked at little Twig. The giving of a name had not helped her a bit. She was thin, fretful, and would not eat the fine broth Sand gave her. The broth was the water Sand boiled the meat and roots in and was very good. Still, as often as not, Twig would throw the bowl away. Sand was dreadfully worried. Many cave babies were like Twig, and they all finally died. When she spoke of it to Ulf, he just said it was good Twig wasn't a boy. Losing a daughter wasn't half as bad as losing a son.

Dog had gone to fetch Bearclaw again, and now the two entered the cave. Bearclaw had one of his precious bags of salt water on his back.

"Bearclaw, can you make her eat?"

"I don't know. We will try this again." He scooped out a little of the water and held it to Twig's lips. She spat it out. Dog watched the whole process. He didn't blame Twig; he didn't like salt water himself. Now if it tasted like broth–there was an idea! Dog took a scoop of the water and dumped it into the bowl of broth.

"Here, sometimes she will eat this. Maybe she won't taste the salt water." Bearclaw nodded. It sounded like good magic. He held the bowl up to her lips, and she gulped it down!

"See! She likes it!" exclaimed Dog. Sand wondered why. She tasted the broth herself. She smiled and handed it to Bearclaw. He tasted it, smacked his lips, and handed it to Dog, who had been jumping up and down impatiently to know what was so wonderful. Bearclaw left that bag at the cave of Ulf and went home to plan an expedition to the sea for more salt water. The men would return the way they went and not by the mountain route. Putting a little salt water in the cooking food was indeed good magic, and therefore it was worth the trip.

Dog didn't go on this expedition. The children were too busy playing with the dugouts that had brought the newcomers. They took two of the big hollow logs, tied them together, and dragged them out to the center of the river where it was deep. They meant to use them to climb upon when they were swimming, but they would always drift away, and the boys would have to swim for all they were worth to catch them again.

It was Shal who thought of what to do. He told the girls to take the dugouts to the middle of the river and to hold them there. The girls clung to the sides and kicked furiously against the current. Meanwhile, the boys brought out all the thongs they could find. They were mystified, for Shal would not tell his idea. He brought a basket he had been making. It was constructed entirely of thongs, and it was quite large. He had not cut off the thongs that pointed into the air! Instead, he had tied the ones opposite each other together, making many loop-like handles over the top of the basket. He fastened the longest thong to the place where these loops crossed.

By the time that was accomplished, Tabat had entered the scene. He was pulling a carrying board with a huge rock tied securely to it.

"This idea better be good," he panted.

Then a difficulty presented itself to Shal. He frowned and scratched his head. "Girls," he called, "I forgot something. Bring those dugouts back."

Dog caught the idea. "I know! I know! But I won't tell!" he shouted, jumping up and down.

The girls scolded Shal all the way in, but Dog said that it was such a fine idea that they shouldn't mind one mistake. He and Shal put the big rock in the center of the two dugouts, where they came together. It was the only place that wouldn't sink them.

"We will have to tow them out again," said Shal, and he picked up the thong arrangement and swam out ahead. As the inventor, he was excused from the hard labor. The rest of the children pushed the heavily laden craft back to the center of the river. They were so curious now they would do anything Shal or Dog said. But Dog had disappeared! Shal grinned and said they'd just have to wait for Dog. The mystery grew when Dog swam back with a flint bore in his mouth!

The two boys started to work. They bored a hole in the front of one of the dugouts, right above the waterline. Through this hole, they tied the free end of the long thong. Now the problem was getting the rock into the basket. The boys tugged and pushed until they had the big stone into one dugout. Oh how that boat tilted! It would go over in a minute!

Dog and Shal hastily pulled apart the loops over the basket and held it ready. They held their breaths as well. The dugout tipped farther and farther. The stone, at last, rolled off the edge and into the basket neatly! The force jerked the contrivances from the boy's hands, and the basket went *glug, glug, glug, glug* as it sank down to the bottom of the river.

Dog and Shal sighed with relief. It had worked! Then they looked at the raft and sighed with despair. Their anchor had pulled the hole Dog bored under the waterline, and the holes on the sides of the dugouts where they were fastened together were also submerged. Both dugouts were full of water!

"Why not turn them upside down?" asked Tabat. "They are flat on the bottom, and we can stand up on them better. We'd have to untie them, turn each one over separately, and then tie them together again."

Tabat and Dog dived underneath
to tie them back together.

Dog laughed. It looked like they would be successful in spite of the mess the raft was now. He climbed into one dugout and untied the connecting thongs. It was up to the girls to keep the other one from drifting away.

"Heave Ho!" the boys called. They pushed the raft up, grunting as they worked. Suddenly there was a splash! It was bottom-side up! They did the same thing to the other one. They pushed it slowly up until they heard a splash! The boats were upside down. Tabat and Dog dove underneath to tie them back together.

When that was finished, they all set up a wild clamor for Bearclaw. He came running and laughed when he saw them. They were pushing each other off, diving, and having all sorts of loud, splashy fun. Bearclaw waved at them.

"Good magic!" he called.

"Hi Yo!" they answered, and Bearclaw sat down upon the riverbank to watch them play. He wondered if he, too, could swim. *It wouldn't hurt anything to try,* he thought and laughed at himself and strode into the water. He went in up to his neck, jumped, and worked his arms and legs the way he saw the children do it. He moved! *Hi Yo!* He could swim! He swam out to the raft, where the astonished children cried, "Why, it's Bearclaw!"

The old man smiled. "Of course. Did you think you were the only ones who could swim? When I was a boy, I lived by a river, and I could swim farther and faster than any other boy in the tribe!"

Dog laughed. "I thought you said once that you lived in the old village of Pang all your life."

"You're right, Dog, but I can swim as well as any of you now!"

Everyone joined in the laugh. They knew Bearclaw was just making the stories up, and they loved to catch him at it. Bearclaw sat on the raft and watched the children play in the water. They stayed until they were cold, and then the whole lot of them swam to shore. Bearclaw told them stories while they sat on the bank and dried off.

Sand was feeding the goats some of the herbs her family didn't eat. There were three goats now. The two original ones had grown up, and there was a young, wobbly kid.

Sand sat Twig, who was still thin and weak despite the salt, on the ground and began to feed the billy goat. Twig looked at the little kid, who was having dinner. She crawled closer to examine his method of eating. Grabbing the fur on the goat's leg, she clutched hard and reared herself up on her feet. She stood there, swaying back and forth. She found she was just high enough to reach, and soon she was drinking as greedily as the kid. It was several minutes before Sand noticed her daughter's activity. When she did see her, she grabbed her away from the goat.

"Drinking goat's milk! You are no animal! Come away!" she cried. Twig began to scream and crawled back to the goat. "Bearclaw!" called Sand, "Bearclaw! Bearclaw! Come here!" There was so much concern in her voice that the old man came running. "Oh, Bearclaw, I am afraid my child is part animal. See how she drinks, just like the little kid!"

"Don't be alarmed, Sand. All animals are made for men to use. Perhaps this is what we have been looking for. Perhaps it is like medicine."

Sand approached the goat cautiously. Bearclaw dumped the bowl of roots and held it to catch the milk. "Smell it," he said. "That cannot be bad magic. Come every day and milk the goat. Do not take it all, but leave some for the kid. Divide the milk with Lin, for her baby is like Twig. I hope these goats multiply rapidly, for the milk smells so good, I believe all men would like to drink it."

Of course, Bearclaw was right. Sand gave him the rest of the milk to take to Lin, and she took Twig, who had already drunk her fill, home. The minute Dog entered the cave, he noticed a change. The continuous, fretful wail was gone, and Twig was gurgling happily in her cradle. Dog had a whole basketful of bird's eggs. He broke a small one, and let it fall into Twig's mouth.

"That's because you are quiet for a while," he said. Twig loved bird's eggs. Ulf noticed it too when he returned from his journey to the sea. They had brought back enough salt water to last the tribe for a year. He entered the cave and looked around. Sand was pouring some white liquid into a bowl, and Twig was actually standing alone, reaching for it! She fell down instantly, but the fact that she had been standing there astounded Ulf.

"What happened?" he asked. "What magic is this? Twig is well!"

"Milk," answered Sand. "Goat's milk. Twig was drinking with the kid, and I was afraid, but Bearclaw said it was good magic. And it was, too. See how strong and fat she is getting, and that wasn't so long ago either!"

Ulf sat down and scratched his head. *Goat's milk...?* It was the strangest thing he had ever heard of. His thoughts were interrupted by Dog and Sky, who threw themselves on their father.

"Fight!" shouted Dog. "I can get you down!"

"Get you down!" laughed Sky.

"Oh, can you?" And the three of them immediately rolled on the floor in a lively wrestling match. Sky would get elbowed out, but he jumped right into it again, and the two boys finally got Ulf on his back.

"You're down! Now I'm chief!" shouted Dog as he stood with one foot on Ulf's chest.

"I chief, too," said Sky, and he planted his foot on Ulf's neck.

"Get up, you three empty heads. See how you have scattered furs all over the cave. Here, Dog, Twig didn't drink all of the milk. You may divide this little bit with Sky." Sand handed Dog the bowl, and he took a big swallow, and then he gave the rest to Sky. Sky got only a little swallow.

"So," said Ulf, "that's what makes you so strong and fierce. I see where I'll have to go into the mountains for more goats."

"No, you shan't. I won't have you crossing any more glaciers or earthquakes."

"We won't go up that high. I think it would be a good idea. It will be many seasons before there will be enough milk for all the babies. I will talk to Bearclaw about it."

"But Ulf, if we have any more goats, how can we keep them here?"

Dog had an answer for that. "Weave a basket around them out of big branches."

"Of course, Sand. Do you see how simple it is? And we can stop at that fruit grove and load up our carrying boards."

Sand said no more. She knew Ulf was set on going, and it would be useless to try to stop him. But she was a little angry at Dog for thinking of a way to keep the goats so easily.

Dog, meanwhile, had heard the children swimming, and he ran out to join them. There was rather a chill breeze in the air that was unusual for midsummer, but he didn't mind that. In he dove and swam out to the raft.

The children played for a long time. Dog stayed in the water even after the others left. He liked the feel of the wetness around him. He pretended he was a fish and swam with his feet together. Pretty soon, he began to shiver a little, so he climbed up on the raft to get warm in the sun. He fell asleep, and though the sun shone brightly, a cold wind swept down the river. In a short while, the sky became cloudy, and a summer shower was in full swing when Dog finally awoke. Dog was cold. He swam back to shore and ran home, shivering and sniffling. The following day, he had a high fever.

As soon as she got up, Sand noticed something was wrong. Dog's face was flushed, and his eyes looked droopy. Every once in a while, he shivered, and he said he didn't want anything to eat. The demons were jumping in his head and stomach, and he ached all over.

"Ulf, go get Bearclaw to make magic over Dog! He's sick!"

Ulf jumped up and was out of the cave in an instant. Dog was his oldest son, and he was sick! Ulf ran into Bearclaw's cave and dragged him out. They ran back through the puddles left by the brief rainfall.

Dog had thrown the covers off of him and sent his fever higher still. By the time Ulf returned with Bearclaw, Dog was delirious. He thought he was Puppy fighting the saber-toothed tiger, and he thrashed around on his bed while every movement made his fever climb higher.

The first thing Bearclaw did was send Twig and Sky over to Tabat's mother to care for them. He knew such demons ran from one person to another, especially in children.

"It is the fire demon sickness," he explained. "They make him hot, and if he gets too hot, he will die. But if we make them hot, then they will die, melt, and come out of his skin. He must lie quiet." Dog, meanwhile, was jumping around on his bed, clawing and biting at the air.

Outside, all the people in Pang were gathered around. Word spread swiftly that the chief's son was sick and the demons were in his mind. Ulf was glad that Bearclaw was their medicine man instead of Fire, for Bearclaw was very wise.

Sand tried to make Dog lie down, but he pushed her across the cave. Bearclaw said that the heat demons gave him the strength of a great man. The only thing to do was to tie him down. He and Ulf together got him on his back, and Sand tied thongs with big rocks on the ends to his wrists, ankles, and another around his waist. Dog roared and yelled, but he couldn't get up. Bearclaw said to cover him with a great bearskin and to place heated rocks on top of that along his sides. Then every other spare skin was to be put on top of that. He told Sand that no matter how Dog shouted or cried, she was not to uncover him and was to keep changing the rocks so they'd always be hot. He told Ulf to build up the fires in the stove and in front of the cave, and with that, he went outside to call the people for a devil dance.

Dog was hot and exhausted. Soon he lay perfectly still with his eyes closed. He breathed heavily through his mouth and looked so stupid and strange that Sand was frightened.

As it was a child that was ill, the other children performed the dance. Bearclaw put on his full devil-chasing regalia and stood at the entrance of Ulf's cave. The children danced around in a circle in front of him. They beat on tom-toms and shook rattles made of clay with nuts inside. Bearclaw's prize demon chaser was a big conch shell Ulf brought him from the sea. At short intervals, he would blow a long, desolate howl upon it. The rest of the people squatted on the ground and swayed back and forth, wailing. They wondered why Bearclaw did not bring Dog down to the glade and hold the dance there. That is what Fire had always done. They forgot that nearly all of Fire's devil dances had failed, and the people had died.

142

It was so hot inside the cave that Ulf and Sand scarcely had enough strength to move. The evening came, but Dog was no better. The dance continued, and Ulf and Sand watched the long shadows leap around on the cave walls and listened to the weird cries.

Dog was awake part of the time, but he didn't know anyone. He kept muttering about riding on the back of the sun mammoth. All night the dance went on, and Dog knew nothing. Just before dawn, he woke up and cried for Sand, but when she came to him, he thought she was Fire and was afraid. Soon, however, he went to sleep again.

"Look!" exclaimed Ulf. "Dog sleeps with his mouth shut! See the drops of water on his face! The demons are leaving!" He ran outside and shouted the glad news to the people just as the sky was turning pink. Before the sun had risen, the happy tribe was home, sleeping off their anxiety from the night before.

Jet came to see Dog, and she brought a
wolf cub for him to play with.

Sand quietly removed the thongs because she knew Dog would lie still now. All day and all that night, Dog slept, and the next morning he blinked and opened his eyes.

"Where's Sky?" he asked. "And why do I have all these covers on? I'm hot."

"You stay right there. You very nearly joined the spirit world, but you are better now. Here, drink this warm goat milk."

She didn't have to coax him to lie still. He felt as though he couldn't even lift the bowl of milk, so he let her hold it. Bearclaw came in, pushed his bed against the wall in a corner, and piled furs at his back so he could sit up a little. Dog wanted his arms out, so Bearclaw took a big pelt and wrapped it around his shoulders. Dog was an absolute chief that day, and he demanded all sorts of attention.

Jet came to see him, and she brought a wolf cub for him. Puppy's pack was growing. Tabat and Fox Ear brought several flattened bones and a sharp tool for carving. Snow brought him a bowl of fine broth, and Shal brought a basket filled with perfectly round pieces of clay painted bright colors. They played a game with Shal's gift called clay balls. Of course, Dog could not play in bed, but this was a most enviable assortment of clay balls, and Shal felt that Dog should have them.

Once the children came, they didn't think of leaving, so Bearclaw came over and told them stories to keep them from wrestling around and ruining the cave and sending Dog back into a fever.

Dog loved this part of being sick. If he thought interest in his well-being was waning, he would immediately demand something, and it would be received. The tribe of Pang was thrilled over this seemingly miraculous driving out of devils, and they discussed it among themselves. "Yes," they would agree. "Bearclaw is a good medicine man. He makes good magic."

Chapter Thirteen:

Fire's Trap

Dog was soon well, but it was early autumn before he was completely strong. By then, he had grown tired of playing clay balls, shooting at a notch cut into a tree, carving, and other milder plays. He longed to run, swim, and climb trees. But when he started any of these activities, he grew tired and weak. His mother made him drink lots of milk, for Ulf and the men had gone after more goats and now had quite a sizable flock. Whenever they took the goats to a grassier place, they found the dogs still knew how to herd. Ulf took several puppies up to the Reindeer tribe, and they were no longer bothered by their animals roaming off. Bearclaw captured some wild pigs and built a very stout stone wall around them. Young pig was very tender eating!

Throughout the summer, the people gathered fruits and berries as they became ripe. Many of these they dried and laid away for winter. Birds' eggs they could not save, but fish and meat could be dried, and they could store the nuts that were beginning to ripen.

Pang was prospering, and far to the north, Fire sat in his cave and cracked his knuckles as he listened to reports of Ulf's good fortune from his sons. If only he could think of a certain way to kill Ulf! For days, he would stare into the fire and mutter to himself. At last, he had a plan, and it seemed it must work. He called his sons and went farther north to a valley he knew abounded with saber-toothed tigers. He dug a pit there.

Back in Pang, the children were gathered on the riverbank, wondering what to do. Dog wanted to take a dugout and paddle across the river to play in the tall whisker grass that was ripening on the opposite bank. His suggestion was adopted with shouts, and he and several others jumped into a dugout while the rest braved the autumn chill and swam. They had never considered crossing the river before, and they were surprised at the height of the wild oats.

"They look something like little nuts, don't they?"

"Let's eat some," challenged Tabat, and acting upon his words, he put one of the whisker grains into his mouth. He chewed the chaff off, spit it out, and ate the oat. It was good. Soon they were all eating oat grains in the same manner as a bird, until Jet calmly picked hers apart with her fingers and then ate it. The rest felt rather silly for not having thought of that.

The children played a primitive form of tag among the wild oats. It was a fine place, for no one could see them when they crawled on hands and knees, and they could creep up behind their victim and knock them over. In Pang Tag, a person had to sit down hard before it was his turn to find someone else to push. They let Sky play too, but they always put him down easy because he was little.

Before they went back across the river, they cut great sheaves of oats and loaded them on the dugout. On the other side, they divided them and took them home. Sand wondered what mischief Dog had been up to when she saw him standing in the cave entrance with the oats over his arm and a foolish grin on his face.

"Well?" she asked.

"I was across the river."

"Across the river! You didn't swim, did you?"

"No, I went in the dugout. See, I have some whisker grass for you. The little nuts are good to eat when you pull the skins off."

Sand examined the whisker grass closely. It would be tedious work to pick each little grain out of its shell. She had a better idea. She spread a big skin on the floor, fur-side down. She laid the oats on it, took a flat bone, and pounded the grains. When she lifted the chaff, there was a neat little pile of shining oats! She ate one and found it as good as Dog said.

"But they are hard, Dog. Too hard to give to Twig, and too small for a meal for the rest of us." She took the bone and pounded the grains again in an effort to soften them. All she accomplished was cracking them open.

"Mother, why not try cooking them? Water softens the hard roots and herbs."

"You're right, Dog. Fetch me that bowl over there–the one with the birds on it." She put in fresh water, salt water, and grains and set them on the stove.

Fire's wife was afraid when he told her he had been to the saber-tooth valley.

"Fire!" she cried, "no one ever goes there and comes back alive."

"Fire can. Fire is a great medicine man. Haven't I already been there once?"

"It won't happen many times."

"Bah! You are an old woman and have no more courage than a tiny field mouse. It's a good thing my sons have courage, or we would never succeed in killing Ulf."

"Why do you want to kill Ulf? He's not harming you now."

At these words, Fire flew into a fit of anger. He yelled until he ran out of breath. When he had quite worn himself out, he threw himself on the most luxurious cot, and shortly the cave was filled with his loud snores.

Meanwhile, to the north and west, a giant saber-toothed tiger was chasing a rabbit across a clearing. The rabbit was too light, but the tiger broke the covering and fell, roaring and spitting, into the pit.

Back in Pang, Sand was amazed at the way the grains swelled. Several times she had to add water, and once, she transferred the cereal to a larger bowl. Dog and Sky watched the operations with interest. Even Puppy sniffed eagerly at the new scent, but he was disappointed. He liked the smell of cooking meat much better.

"Puppy," said Dog, "let's go and get some nuts." The dog jumped on his master, barked, and whined in eagerness at the words 'Puppy, let's go.' He woke Twig up, and she started to cry. Sand chased Dog and Puppy out of the cave.

The two pals looked sheepishly at each other. Dog grabbed a basket, and they started toward the woods. Dog sang to Puppy.

The leaves are falling in the woods.

Puppy doesn't care.

He snaps at them and thinks they're fun.

The wind is beginning to bite with cold.

Puppy doesn't care.

His coat grows warm and thick and protects him.

Soon the hungry wolves will be howling near Pang.

Puppy doesn't care.

He's a dog now and would rather be with me.

Hi Yo! Puppy! Go and get that rabbit!

Wide Eye, the spy, heard the song and knew the singer. He hurried away before they discovered him.

When the basket was full of nuts, they went home. Sand had put Twig to sleep again. When Dog and Puppy ambled into the cave, they didn't notice a large stone on the floor. Of course, Dog tripped and fell over Puppy, who yelped in pain as the basket of nuts went flying across the cave. The combined noises had barely stopped when there arose a small wail from the cradle that steadily increased in volume.

"Oh, you clumsies!" scolded Sand. "Everywhere you go, you make a disturbance. Aren't you ashamed?"

"Yes, Mother." Dog went over to his cot and sat down. Puppy followed, his ears down and his tail between his legs. Still, on his face, there was a mischievous grin. He and Dog had been naughty, and he knew it, but the nuts had made a very pleasant din, and Sand wasn't really angry.

Sand stirred the oatmeal with a slender bone. It was beginning to soften a little, and Sand noticed the whole grains remained solid while the cracked ones cooked. Next time she would have to put them into a hollow stone and grind them.

When Ulf came in that night, she served him a bowl of the new food. The children liked it. It was too thin to pick up and eat like meat and too thick to drink like broth, so Dog fashioned thin flat bones with a round hollow in one end. Sand gave it to Ulf and told him to eat. He tasted it.

"It is no good! Only fit for children!" he said, emptying the dish on top of the stove where the cereal began to bubble. It stuck, and Sand had to use a knife to scrape it off. She lifted it on the knife's blade; it flipped and turned over, leaving the brown side on top! It smelled different and very appetizing. Ulf took the knife and picked up the flat cake. He rolled it and took a bite.

"Good! This is the way to give it to a man!" he exclaimed.

Sand made one each for Dog, Sky, and herself. Twig would have to eat it the other way for a while.

The other women had merely shelled their grains and let the children eat them. One woman stood her sheaf outside the door of her hut, where many grains fell to the earth, unnoticed. When Sand told them of the many things they could make with the whisker grass, the people crossed the river and cut the whole field. The job took many days, for they were clumsy at it. Great quantities of grain fell while they were cutting. That was lucky for the tribe, for it meant more oats the next year. They threshed the oats a little at a time and put the grain in baskets to store it over the winter.

Dog was fond of taking a handful and eating them like nuts. Sand caught him once, and Ulf administered a spanking. Dog went outside and sulked while Sand hung the basket up high so he couldn't reach it. Puppy licked his ears in sympathy, but Dog was angry at the world. He gave Puppy a push and told him to go away. Puppy did, but he was very sad about it.

Sky asked Dog to tell him a story, but Dog refused. Why should he bother? He threw a rock into a flock of birds that were pecking at the ground. He wished they'd hurry up and go to the warm lands. At that moment, he hated everything. Sand left him alone. She knew he'd get over his sulking when he smelled food on the stove.

Fire and his sons were gathered at the tiger pit. The great beast below was raging at them and trying to get out.

"Here he is. Now what do we do?" asked Wide Eye. Fire glared at him. The problem of getting the tiger out of the pit alive had been bothering him, and he didn't like to have it brought up aloud. Also, the abundance of saber-toothed tigers in this valley made him nervous. He wanted to get out as soon as possible.

He saw a good-sized rock laying nearby, and it inspired him. He carried it to the edge of the pit and threw it at the tiger. It hit the beast squarely on the head, and he fell unconscious. Two of his sons were lowered into the pit.

Sky asked Dog to tell him a story, but he refused.

152

They tied the tiger's jaws together and trussed him to a pole. They fastened thongs to each end of the pole so it would be easy to get out. The tiger was most uncomfortable when he came to. He was hanging on a pole, and the hated man-scent was all around. He was helpless. He couldn't even roar!

Back in Pang, Dog was over his sulk, just as Sand had expected. He came inside and told Sky the story of the earthquake. Sky had heard it many times before, but it never lost its awe-inspiring interest. That may have been because it got better every time Dog told it. At that telling, when Dog fainted and fell over the edge of the cliff, he came to just in time to grab a vine and swing himself back to the ledge.

Sand stopped this outrage by announcing that the meat was cooked and that they had to hurry if anybody wanted to eat. Ulf laughed at her, but he hurried. When the family members were satisfied, they sat around and watched Ulf carve a saber-toothed tiger on the cave wall. He already had a picture of Puppy and wanted to finish the story. The family of Ulf went to sleep when it was quite dark, and the stars couldn't tell them of the procession that was coming closer and closer.

It was Fire and his sons carrying the tiger. The tiger had learned the scent of the big man with the thong that stung. Against that man before all others, his fury mounted. Fire chuckled to himself as he thought of the gory end he had planned for Ulf and his whole family. Perhaps even the entire village!

They crept silently into Pang and to the top of Ulf's cave. Directly below them was the entrance. They pushed the pole out over the edge and put a big boulder on the end to hold it. They cut the bonds from the tiger's hind feet. There he hung in the entrance to Ulf's cave while Ulf slept! They cut the bonds around his mouth, and he roared. That would wake the whole village–they'd have to work fast. Fire, himself, cut the thongs from the tiger's front paws and ran, not even looking back to watch him fall, fear-maddened, in front of his enemy's cave!

The roar woke Ulf, who saw the two yellow legs and the long, switching tail hanging in the entrance. He saw the legs claw, finally get a hold, and disappear over the edge! The sabertoothed tiger had not fallen, but the animal had caught onto the bank! Up he crawled

and went after the one man he had learned to hate! Straight toward the happy witch doctor, he ran. Fire was strolling leisurely up the path. He would have to return soon and see how wonderful Ulf looked dead!

Suddenly Fire screeched, and his sons ran for their lives. The medicine man's fiendish plot had been like a boomerang! The tiger caught up with him and leaped on his back in the darkness. One sweep of the giant paw–one bite with the giant fangs–and Fire was dead! He died from his own wicked plot to kill someone else.

The tiger turned from Fire's body to face a ring of Ulf's warriors with flaring torches. He cowered in the face of the flames, afraid to leap. An arrow struck him and another and another. He walked in a circle snarling and seeking an opening in the ring of fire. Then an arrow struck a vital spot, and the tiger fell dead across the body of Fire! The men brought the tiger home, but left Fire there.

"He was very wicked. Do not bury him, but leave him for the demons to carry off," counseled Bearclaw, and the tribe went back to talk of the strange thing that happened in the night. Ulf was glad Fire was dead, and he was also glad that he did not have to kill him. Ulf hated killing.

Ulf found Dog waiting for him. He had told his son to stay in the cave and protect Sand, Sky, and Twig in case something else should happen. This made Dog feel very important, but he would much rather have gone where the excitement was. Toward dawn, Fire's sons came and bore their father's body to the north. They buried and built a cairn over him in the cave where they had lived because of him. Everyone looked at it silently for several minutes, and then Wide Eye spoke.

"We have done our duty in serving him while he was alive, and keeping the demons from taking his body now that he is dead. Let us go to the Reindeer tribe and make peace so we can have a home among humans again." The others nodded and picked up their belongings. A day later, Dar was listening to their tale, and he accepted them and gave them an empty cave to live in. There they remained and caused no more trouble. They had already had enough to last a lifetime.

Dog and Tabat were having a fine game of clay balls. They drew a circle in the dirt and laid a row of clay balls across it. Then they drew a wider circle farther out, and each boy sat on opposite sides of the circle and took turns shooting at the center. The clay balls they knocked out of the little circle they won. Dog was winning all of Tabat's clay balls, and Tabat was grumbling. It seemed Dog's pouch was bottomless, and it would take every one of his clay balls to fill it. Dog was jubilant and laughed at Tabat's inability–until Tabat began to win, and Dog's pouch became limper and limper. Then he was sad and Tabat glad. That sort of thing went on for the greater part of the afternoon, and when they finished, each had about the same number of clay balls he had started with.

That night the whole village was to gather around the council fire and hear the story of Fire's death and the killing of the saber-toothed tiger. Dog and Tabat beat on the tom-tom, and the people gathered–blonde and redheaded alike–the whole mighty tribe of Pang. The children sat in a group in front of Bearclaw. The entire wolf pack was there, too, with their little masters. Puppy was asleep with his head in Dog's lap. Sky was sitting on the other side of Dog with his eyes wide. He was doing his best to keep from following Puppy's impolite example. Tabat sat next, then Fox Ear and Shal. Jet and Snow were together, and they whispered altogether too much.

Bearclaw put a drop of milk, a piece of dried meat, a dried fruit, a nut, and an oat on a little carved wooden dish. Those made the fall offering to the fire god so that they would have an easy winter. Then he told the great story, and the people danced the torch dance. Dog, Sky, Sand, Twig, Puppy, and Knife Tooth followed Ulf, the chief, home. They were tired and sleepy, and tomorrow there would be so many pleasant things to do and time to play!

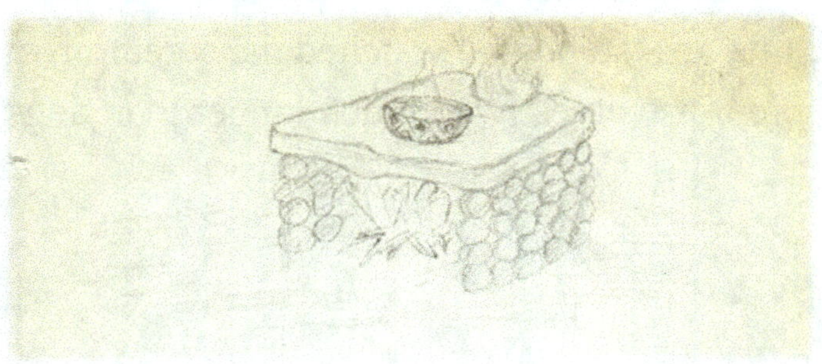

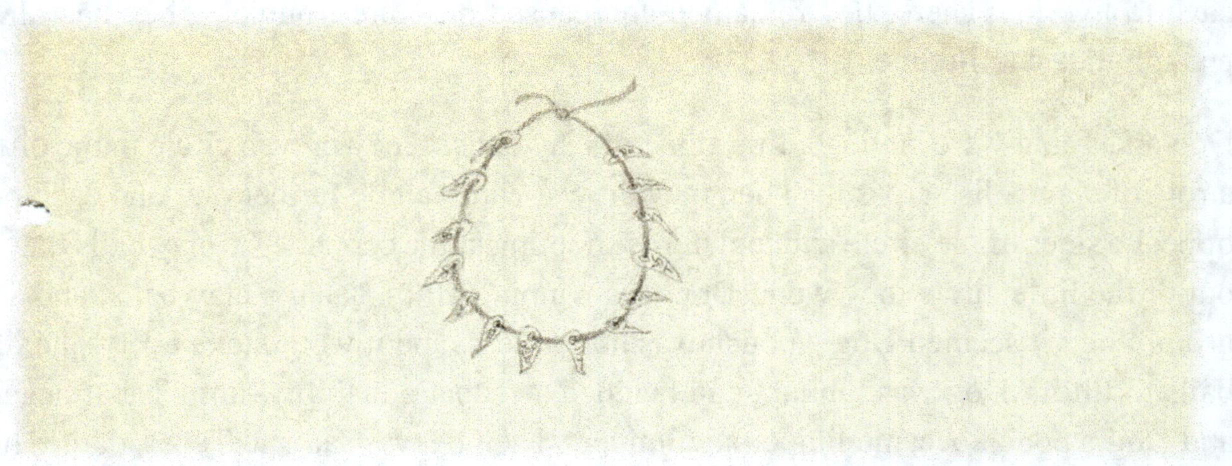

Chapter Fourteen:

Dog Grown Up

Years passed. They were happy and pleasant years for the tribe of Pang. The men and boys hunted and fought, and the men grew old as the boys grew to manhood. Dog was twenty years old. He had built himself a fine hut with a large stove. His wife, Jet, must have the best! Nearby, Tabat also erected a hut and brought his wife there to live. He had married Snow.

One day, old Bearclaw joined his ancestors in the spirit world, and Ulf was given the headdress of the medicine man. Dog had been the boy's leader for so many years that it was perfectly natural for him to be made chief. The carved necklace seemed to have been made for his neck. Ulf was very proud when he gave his honors to Dog, and Sky kept telling everyone, as if they didn't already know, "That's my brother!" Sand and Twig, who was growing into a tall, fine girl, stood and watched the ceremony with tears of joy in their eyes. Even Puppy was there, for wolves lived much longer than dogs do now.

Ulf was very proud when
he gave his honors to Dog.

Dog was a good chief, and his people loved him. He relied on the wise council of Ulf, and the people were glad to see that he was not overly proud. Many strange tribes tried to invade Pang during Dog's chieftainship, but each tried it only once. Far and wide went Dog's fame as the Great Wolf Chief because of the huge pack of fierce watchdogs that accompanied him and his warriors into every battle. It was Dog, remembering the fight with the invaders, who devised a wood framework with skins stretched taut across it to deflect arrows.

It had been a northern woman who noticed so many years ago that the oats growing outside her hut had appeared where the grains had dropped the year before. Now every spring, the women spread seeds in the old oat field. The women learned that they did not have to scrape the flat cake from the stone if they mixed the oatmeal with some animal fat. Also, it made the cake crispy and gave it a new good taste. The people kept their milk in goatskin bags. Jet hung hers on a branch of a tree. One day her oldest son used it as a sort of punching bag. When she looked at the milk, she found it full of yellow lumps. She tasted them and found they were good. The tribe of Pang had butter from then on.

Dog had the same urge that made Ulf wander. He took many trips and had many adventures. Each time he returned to Pang, he always brought a new form of good magic with him. The people began to say Dog was even greater than old Pang himself! He established peace for miles around Pang, and a man could go alone on a trading venture if he wished, and the only danger would be from animals.

And when men told stories to their children, they would love to point to their wise chief and tell the story of Crazy Dog and the Wolf.